ENCOUNTER

ENCOUNTER

By Ivy Ruckman

DOUBLEDAY & COMPANY, INC.
GARDEN CITY, NEW YORK

ISBN: 0-385-14150-5 Trade
0-385-14151-3 Prebound
Library of Congress Catalog Card Number 77–26519

For Bret,
who also is seventeen and perceptive

ENCOUNTER

ONE

"Stephanie!" JD yelled back at the house. "Get your stuff out here!" He drew himself up to his full six feet two—impressive for a high school senior—then let his shoulders settle into slouch position again. Gloomily, he faced the mound of camping gear piled by the Volkswagen.

He remembered how his dad threw it all together in the back of the pickup, pulling a tarp over the grub sacks and sleeping bags, then surveying the whole with an eye practiced in compromise. "That'll do." It was his old man's philosophy. JD found himself smiling. "It'll do. It'll work. Good enough." JD had other ideas for himself, but now, at the last minute, he wasn't sure taking his sister along to the Gorge was one of them. It was bad enough when his buddy Chic couldn't go, but then to have Stephanie beg him to take *her*—man, how she'd begged!

"Coming!" Stephanie yelled from the upstairs window.

Sooner than he expected she was standing beside him, loaded down with her faded red parka, a duffel bag, and an oversized Snoopy pillow.

"Steph, you're not taking that . . . that *security blanket*," he lifted the pillow out of her arms and plopped it on top of the trunk in disgust.

"I am, JD!"

Stephanie's blue eyes were sending out the same determined vibrations they had the night before. "I won't be in your way at the Gorge," she'd pleaded. "Please. Puleeze, JD! I never get to go anywhere!" He knew there was no use to argue with her now, either. He'd have had to compress the Snoopy pillow into some corner even if it was elephant size.

Stephanie turned happily and bounced back to the house for another load. Her blue-jeaned bottom was worth a second look, JD mused, feeling vaguely pleased, even in defeat, to be this fifteen-year-old's brother.

Half an hour later, after being hugged and kissed, they were on their way, their mother's warnings ringing in their ears: "You watch out for snakes . . . keep your feet dry, Stephanie . . . and don't talk to strangers, you hear?"

The Gorge was a two-hour drive from Red Butte, the Wyoming town where the two Anderson kids had moved with their parents four years before. Each time now, the trips to the mountain were for JD like a return to the ranch. He had the same feelings about both places: that there was something honest and solid and real out *there* that he didn't find in town. He could close his eyes and see the home place—the gray buildings huddled together in a sea of sage, the stand of poplars running right up to a lazy bend in the Platte. It gave him goose bumps.

But he knew the same wasn't true with Stephanie. She couldn't remember half the fun they'd had as kids, swilling the hogs with Dad's best Bourbon, setting the haystack afire one glorious day. He'd name off their pet calves—Clover, Dynamite, Pushbutton. No luck. The only heifer that came to her mind had chewed up the skirt of her starched Sunday dress—while she was in it! JD had laughed so hard: the salivating calf, working the yardage into its mouth until the pink gingham stretched tight across her back, and Stephanie, standing there stiff as a board, calf slobber running down her legs, screaming with rage . . .

One vision they did share from those ranch years was Steph trying to out-streak the rooster who chased her home from the hen house every day. She'd dash for the side gate of the yard, her kindergarten legs pumping like pistons. If she made it with all the eggs intact, she patted herself on the back all day.

Sometimes, JD thought Stephanie had suppressed that earlier time, like the book in Psych II said people often did. Their lives were a lot softer after moving to Red Butte, anyway. Now Steph was growing up to be some woman, he could see that if he worked at it. Under the stubbornness, she was all heart.

"What are you thinking about? And how far are we?" Stephanie asked, squirming to find a spot of comfort. She'd been reading for over an hour and now she tossed the paperback assignment on the floor of the car. "*Oedipus Rex!* Yuk!" It was a death pronouncement.

"Which question do you want answered first?"

"Number two, then *numero uno,*" she smiled, pulling up her knees and hooking her chin over her hands.

JD took his time. He liked to give considered answers. Judging from the red Sundance formation he saw in the road cuts, they were just beginning the ascent, so they wouldn't see timber for the better part of an hour.

"It'll be uphill for forty minutes. Then we'll leave the road

11

and camp back in the aspen a few miles where Dad and I always stayed."

"Do you think he'll ever hunt again?" Stephanie asked abruptly.

She's already forgotten the other question, JD thought.

"Is he just going to get worse? His coughing's terrible." She wouldn't let go. It was one of her traits.

"I don't know, Steph. Emphysema's bad, but Dad's slowed down a lot. Maybe if he takes care of himself . . ."

The conversation gave way to private thoughts as the VW carved through one geological formation after another along the lonely wind-swept highway. JD couldn't imagine hunting without his dad. He heard again the elder John David's words with his mother when he'd come home from the hospital. "Hell, Addie, I'd rather be dead than have to give up hunting and fishing. What's left in life for a man? Running a laundromat, for Chrissake?"

Then, finally, this year, giving up . . . or giving in. JD didn't know what to make of it.

"I won't be deer hunting," his dad said late one night in September, sitting at the kitchen table with JD. "Go on up with some of the guys."

Maybe it was because his dad had looked so haggard that night, or because the lid of his tobacco tin had clattered to the floor just as JD opened his mouth to protest. Instead, he'd only nodded and gone upstairs to bed. He knew he wouldn't join the hunt without his dad. Not this year, anyway.

"I refuse to read one more word of Sophocles while we're camping!"

Stephanie's mind had gone full circle again, JD thought. Now it was back to *Oedipus*.

"The teachers all go off to Cheyenne to their big, hairy

convention and we end up with the homework," she complained.

"Ah, they just get together and booze it up," JD added, like he knew something she didn't.

"Do you think they do?" Stephanie wrinkled her nose. "I mean, someone like Garth? Do you think he really gets stoned at teacher's convention?"

"Aw, I dunno. He's pretty straight."

"How about ol' Miss McGinnis? I *know* she wouldn't."

"She's the one who needs to the most," JD chuckled.

It took them some time to go through the whole faculty of their consolidated high school and some judgment trying to decide who would and who wouldn't.

"Hey, we're here," JD pointed off to a rutted trail coming into the state road at right angles. "See the sign? Skull Mountain."

"Do we camp up on top?"

"No, there's a clearing, two or three hundred yards across. Dad and I always made camp on the west side next to an aspen grove. You'll see."

The VW bounced and swayed. JD slowed to a crawl to avoid the high centers caused by the sheep trucks. This whole side of the mountain had been designated a range study area, and both rangers and ranchers came in and out driving heavy rigs.

It wasn't until they stopped to let themselves through a gate that they noticed the camper parked off to the left among the trees.

"Hey, Steph, we've got company," JD said quietly. He frowned. Two weeks before the hunt. He didn't think anyone would be in here. But as soon as JD got out of the car and uncoiled, feeling the rush of cool air in his face, he decided it didn't matter. They'd be a mile apart, anyway. He swung open the gate.

"Drive her through," he waved at Stephanie, feeling expansive. At home he'd only let her move his car up and down the driveway. Aside from getting flattened himself as she bore down on him, he couldn't see any reason why she shouldn't have the pleasure this time.

As usual, he'd underestimated his sister. She drove it through all right, but she kept going, veering off into the sage, riding the crests of the ruts dangerously, going way too fast. He thought she'd never stop.

"Damn you!" he puffed when he finally caught up with the car. He shoved her over into the passenger seat, ignoring her screams.

"I really do hate you," she retorted, laughing so hard she could hardly get it out.

"It's a love-hate," he teased, smacking her a good one on the near shoulder. He hoped it hurt a little.

"It's a *hate* hate! A capital H hate!" She looked like she might try to clop him right back, but she didn't.

When they rounded the last bend into the clearing JD let out a wild whoop of joy. His heart pounded; a wide grin took over his face. JD was out of the car before it quit rolling. If Stephanie hadn't been along he'd have hugged a tree or something.

"This is it," he was fairly singing. "This is our same old place." JD was jumping from one spot to another. "We dug the latrine behind those junipers over there. That was my job. Hey, look, Steph!" She was stretching beside the car. "Our buck pole from last year. That's where Old Albert hung overnight." He and his dad always gave their deer names. A kind of requiem.

"It's nice here," Stephanie agreed. She stood on her tiptoes and inhaled noisily. "I like it."

JD strode out into the clearing, his hands in his hip pockets, trying to take in everything at once. He'd never seen the mountain this early in October and it was beautiful. Here and there scrub brush and sumac clumps vied for top billing with their fiery oranges and reds. A few aspen leaves still clung to white branches. Like gold pieces, JD thought, hoarding the sunlight. Turning full circle, he could see a higher mountain across the state road where the pines grew so thick they looked blue.

"What d'you think?" He walked back to the car. "This is a great place to camp, isn't it?"

"It's perfect," Stephanie shivered, "but in a minute I'll need my parka."

JD glanced at his watch as they unpacked the car. It was almost four o'clock. There'd be little chance to see elk today. If he could get the picture Crawford wanted for the *Times*, the money would take care of his gas. That way he could get his car payment in on time, too.

"You're an enterprising kid," Crawford had said when JD approached him about getting some shots of the elk herd. "First thing I know you'll be wanting my job!"

It had the ring of truth. JD hung around the office of the *Red Butte Times*—their small town weekly—as much as he dared. He hoped next summer that Crawford could hire him. Being bus boy at the Holiday Inn might pay for his Volks, but it wasn't exactly his choice for a life's work.

JD checked his camera and put it back in its case for the night, then closed the trunk of the car. He'd have to chop up a pile of wood before dark and help Stephanie with some dinner. She was a rotten cook. She'd tackled building the lean-to with so much enthusiasm he thought he might just assign her to dig the latrine. Digging the shit hole made a good initiation. Meanwhile, *he'd* heat the stew and make the coffee.

You were cheated out of evening on Skull Mountain, JD remembered. One minute it was late afternoon, the next time you turned around it was dark. He used to imagine that the sun went down with a "thud" at deer camp. The soft gradations of the sky they were used to seeing in Red Butte, the pinks and oranges of an autumn sunset savored perhaps by the sheepherders on the other side of the mountain, were lost here.

JD built up the fire one last time after dinner. "We'll turn in early," he said as he dragged another log on the coals. For the first time, he noticed how much Stephanie looked like their mother—her long hair braided out of the way with the loose strands forming a halo around her face in the firelight. Both of them blonde, their Scandinavian looks belied their strength. Stephanie, easygoing and strong-backed, had been as good a companion today as he could hope for. Well, except for Gayle Evans. For some reason, though, he didn't associate Gayle with work. With crawling in his sleeping bag maybe. Funny, he hadn't thought of her all day. He wondered what she'd be like on an overnight.

"Are there bears up here?" Steph's voice, sounding smaller than usual, cut her back to kid-sister size in a hurry. She offered JD some of her beer nuts, like her generosity might make for a favorable answer. "Now tell me the truth!"

"There are. But hell, they're just little black bears. We never saw any in camp before."

"What difference does the color make?"

"Don't sweat it. I'll keep the ax in the lean-to. You'll be snug as a bug."

"Ooh, bugs. Earwigs!" she squealed. He ignored her, loading their food supplies back in the car. Stephanie the Novice liked to put on a good show.

Half an hour later they crawled in their sleeping bags. Fully clothed in their jeans and parkas, Stephanie complained again. "I feel like a sausage! How do we sleep so stuffed in like this?"

"Well, try. We're going to be up at daybreak."

In minutes, Stephanie was breathing in long regular draughts of sleep. JD was glad she'd fallen off so easily. The night was dark. With no sign of a moon, JD himself felt uneasy. But why should he be afraid—the senior authority, the protector, the experienced camper? He shuddered as the cold deepened.

TWO

Stephanie with the lunch pack and JD carrying his camera reached the beaver dam early the next morning. It was a three-mile hike, easy because they followed the power lines, but she was beginning to lag. "Wait up!" she yelled at her brother, who was fast disappearing down the deer trail he was following.

Stephanie wasn't sure JD even heard her. Sometimes he could be so exasperating. She tried again.

"Hey, mountain man. Wait up!" she put a good bit of holler in it this time and he turned around, at least. He motioned for her to be quiet. She froze. Minutes passed, but she was glad for the breather. The October sun was already hot on her back. She carefully slipped off her parka and stood waiting for a signal from JD.

Then she saw them. The elk. A cow with her little one, coming to drink. "Oh, they're beautiful!" she said, catching her breath. "And they don't even know I'm here." A new movement caught her eye as an enormous bull, balancing a rack of record proportions, came out of the trees and down through the meadow. Cautiously, he joined the other two at the stream that flowed out of the beaver dam.

She spotted JD. He was so close! He could easily get a picture. "And they're posing," Stephanie marveled. "They're grouped. Like they know." She felt like clapping her hands. She had stupid impulses, JD often told her, but how she wanted to rush up and pet them!

Down from her, frozen to his vantage point, JD felt a trembling start in his diaphragm which became a shudder when it reached his shoulders. He set the distance and the aperture of the camera, all without inhaling, then in a slow motion sequence that stopped at every frame, he fixed his eye at the view finder. Click. The sound shattered his eardrums. Then click. And click again.

The calf looked up and flicked its ears at JD, before prancing sideways with a stiff-legged gait. The bull elk, too, raised his head, testing the air. Then, as silently as they'd come, they slipped away. With an imperial glance over his shoulder, the big bull sauntered after his women folk, pausing only once to crop the grass and enjoy the sun. Soon they were lost in the depths of the aspen again. It was like a disappearance act.

JD came running back up the game trail they'd followed to the dam. He's thrilled right out of his skin, Stephanie thought.

"Did you see that? God, what luck! I can sell these to the *National Geographic!*"

"Really! How many'd you get?"

"Three . . . or four. I don't know. I was so damned nervous. Did you see how they stood there and looked right at me? I wasn't thirty feet away, Stephanie!"

He grabbed her in a bear hug and swung her around, crushing her against his camera until she forced him away in self-defense. Then he was off on a dead run back toward the beaver dam. "Come on," he beckoned, "we're just getting started."

Stephanie laughed, too, as she ran after him. She liked ol'
JD. He got so excited about everything. She couldn't imagine
having a dull sort for a brother. JD was the most colorful, interesting, entertaining person she'd ever known. Of course he
was a hard driver, she thought, scrambling up on the dam
after him. It would be nothing to end the day scratched,
bruised and blistered. Already her legs were sending up signals. But she'd been tagging along behind JD for about thirteen years and she didn't intend to miss anything now.

The two of them spent most of the day crouching behind
the beaver dam. It was at least seventy-five feet long and aban-
doned, they decided, when no beavers were to be seen. Only a
trickle of water escaped to irrigate the green marshy bottom
of the clearing. By the tracks and deer runs they knew this
was a popular watering hole for game and small critters as
well.

At midafternoon they ate their oranges back in the under-
growth, keeping the sun behind them, hoping still to catch an
elk herd before they had to leave.

He's getting gloomy, Stephanie thought later as they stirred
themselves from their hiding place. A cool breeze had made
their parkas feel good again, and when she could no longer
distinguish the bright fall colors from the dingy ones she
knew they'd soon be heading back to camp.

"I'm sorry, JD," she offered as they bundled their food
scraps. "I was sure we'd see a whole bunch of them."

"A herd," he corrected her, frowning. "A herd, Stephanie."

"Yeah, yeah," she had to tolerate his superior airs. "Maybe
tomorrow, huh?" she added, encouragingly, pushing herself
to keep stride with him.

Tomorrow. Sunday. Their last day. JD suspected that
Stephanie didn't want this trip to end any more than he did.
For him, at least, the weekend had had a special quality. The

pressures were gone. It didn't matter if they talked or not. It was almost as if time had been caught, suspended.

Stephanie, too, had been wishing she could seal their sun-drenched day in a mason jar to keep forever. She had a very strong feeling that this might be the best time—the last private time—they'd have together. Next fall he'd be—who knew where? Off to school if he had his way. Northwestern University School of Journalism, maybe, if he got the big scholarship. Laramie if he didn't. Married, even. He and Gayle were getting serious. Anyway, he wouldn't be out crashing through the underbrush with her.

JD and Stephanie had left the smooth, broad cut under the power lines to take a shorter way back to their campsite. Mostly uphill, it was harder hiking, but JD said they could pare twenty minutes off the time it took. Finally, just as Stephanie decided they were lost, they caught sight of the yellow VW through the trees. Even JD looked relieved to find camp where it was supposed to be. Now her legs were really screaming, but she'd have to keep it to herself.

"Hey, I'll race you," JD grinned.

Yeah, he knows I'm dragging, Stephanie thought, but she broke out ahead of him anyway, leaping over fallen logs and dodging the clumps of sage. It was hopeless. JD was two yards ahead of her in no time.

"You win," she panted and threw herself full length on her sleeping bag. "I've had it!"

"Oh, no," JD laughed and poked her with the toe of his boot, "losers chop wood."

"Oh yeah? Then winners cook dinner!" she shot back at him.

In a little more than an hour, thanks to JD, they were eating their bowls of chili by a crackling campfire. The lantern hanging in the tree was the only other light warding off the deepening night. Stephanie wondered how cozy they must look from the line of trees across the clearing. Maybe the elk were watching *them*. She liked the idea.

"You're a great cook, JD," she stood to get a second helping.

"So why can't you chop wood worth a damn?" he countered.

"I'm too fragile. And I haven't been getting any rest lately."

"Yeah, uh-huh. How're you going to feel in the morning about five-thirty?"

"Oh no, JD! Why so early? It's our last day. Let's sleep in!" He's crazy, she said to herself.

"We're going two miles over the ridge in the other direction. We'll never see anything if we don't get out before daylight."

She could tell that was his last word. She wouldn't dare argue. He'd just go off without her. Stephanie poured them both more hot chocolate and set the pot back on the rocks bordering the fire. They finished dinner with a sack of doughnuts and cleaned up their mess in a hurry. It was getting cold and all Stephanie could think about was the toasty warm sleeping bag. Tonight, she wouldn't even feel the lumps under the ground tarp.

JD, methodical as ever, spent more time than necessary, Stephanie thought, getting his gear piled inside the lean-to for their early departure. "Camera, flashlight, billfold, keys," he named them over. Finally, he doused the fire and crawled

into his bag. Stephanie sighed. She felt vastly comfortable.
Even the little night sounds didn't keep her from sleep.

The next thing Stephanie remembered was dreaming about
a fire. It had blazed up during the night, it seemed, and
spread across the clearing. The entire mountainside was in
flames. She woke up gasping and raised herself on one elbow.
She squinted across at JD, trying to end the scary dream by
waking up completely.

But as soon as she opened her eyes she was flooded with
terror. It was no dream! She could see the power poles, three
hundred yards away, as plain as by day. Their car, the wood
pile, the aspen right up to the tree tops were bathed in red
light. Skull Mountain was on fire!

"Oh, God, we've gotta get out of here," she twisted her
arms out of the bag and grabbed at JD.

"Quick, wake up . . . Oh, God, please!" she was praying
now and her heart was pounding in her ears.

"Huh?" he rolled over to face her. "Is it time?"

"JD! Look!" The red had intensified.

"What's a matter? Stephanie, quit it!" She was pulling
him out of the bag, shaking him hard.

"Fire, JD! It's on fire!"

Suddenly he was up, up and out of the lean-to, his face the
color of her fears.

"My God, Steph, what is it?" He stood rigid, staring, his
face contorted.

"Help me!" Stephanie struggled with the zipper of her bag.
"I can't get out!"

JD ducked back into the lean-to, pulled her to her feet, and
peeled the bag down to her ankles. "What is it?" he kept asking, tugging her out of the lean-to so she could see.

Stephanie clutched at JD's arm, unable to breathe. She couldn't believe what was happening. There *was* no fire! Only this strange thing, full of orange light, eerily turning night into day—

"Get your shoes," JD ordered suddenly, already pulling on his boots. "Hurry!"

They ran toward the shelter of the trees behind them. Thirty feet into the aspen, they fell down behind a clump of juniper. Stephanie had never been so terrified.

"Is it the end of the world?" her voice shook wildly.

JD stared open-mouthed, squinting at the great ball of light which seemed to hover right over the power lines. Stephanie's next thought was that the moon had exploded and part of it was hanging there. Then it began to move. In a graceful, floating motion it passed into the clearing, nearer to them than it was before. They couldn't take their eyes off it. Now Stephanie could see blue and green and white lights, individually, pulsing on and off along the center of the sphere, faster than a heart beat.

JD's voice was calmer when he finally spoke. She could see he was trying hard to control himself.

"It's a UFO, Steph. It's gotta be a UFO!"

"From space?" she whispered desperately, still clinging to his parka.

"I don't know," he shook her off his arm and raised up on his knees. "God, how do I know?" They huddled together for several more minutes watching the thing gently lower itself on the far side of the clearing. "What else could it be?"

Stephanie's mind raced for explanations.

"Will you stay here and not move?" JD broke in. "I'm going to get a picture of it."

"Oh no, JD. Please don't go! I'm scared. I can't stand it!"

"Steph, look," he grabbed her face between his hands. "Nothing's going to happen. It's just sitting out there. I'll get a picture and come right back." He was talking fast. "Now stay here. You'll be all right."

"No, JD," she started to cry.

"Look at my hands," he held them out for her to see. "I'm as scared as you, but I've gotta get a picture. Don't you understand? We may be the only ones to see this. Just wait here. You're safe!"

Stephanie held onto his legs, but he was up and away from her before she could stop him. Wiping her face on one sleeve and then the other, she tried to swallow back the sobs that kept coming. Clumsily, she pulled on her heavy shoes, but her hands shook so she could hardly tie the laces.

When she looked again she could see JD's silhouette. He had his camera and was crouching behind the car. Then he was running, and ducking down, then running again toward the thing. Why was he going so close? He was too close! Afraid to call out, she bit down hard on her fist, fighting back the tears that blurred everything into a red, throbbing mass in front of her. Suddenly, she was aware of the low humming sound she'd heard in her dream. How long had that . . . that UFO been watching them?

Wiping her eyes with both hands, she scrambled to her feet, trying to keep track of JD. He must be down. She couldn't see him. "JD," she screamed. She couldn't help it. Where was he? She couldn't see him anywhere, though the light still illuminated every blade of grass in the clearing. "JD!" she yelled again, ready to explode.

Now that JD was gone, maybe in danger, Stephanie forgot herself. She rushed from her hiding place out into the clearing, but beyond the safety of cover, she froze. Alone, a perfect target in the wash of light from the strange craft, she couldn't take another step. Her eyes darted back and forth across the clearing. There was no sign of JD.

Suddenly, she remembered the camper they'd seen when they drove in. She'd get help! She'd take the car and get help. Stephanie whirled around and raced back to the trees.

"Please, God, let somebody be there!" she cried seconds later as she scrambled among JD's things in the lean-to for the keys. Before she left the shelter, Stephanie once again closed her eyes and strained to hear her brother's voice, his footsteps, *anything*. There was no sound at all, but the drumming in her own head.

She ran to the car, but once inside, her hands shook so she could hardly find the ignition. What next? Clutch in. Gearshift in neutral. She turned the key. Nothing. Again and again she twisted the key into starting position. She tried the lights. Nothing. She leaped out of the car.

She had to get help. Still there was no sign of JD and now the thing was beginning to move. To spin. *Something* was spinning—and the humming had started again. It grew so bright she couldn't look at it. She ran headlong down the mountain road, knowing she was without any protection. She willed herself to get to the camper before something happened.

"Run, run, run," she said over and over, pushing until she thought her lungs would burst and then collapsing behind the trees, afraid but compelled to look back. The red light had changed to a strange whitish color—and the thing was rising straight up in the air.

"No!" she screamed, "they've got him!" Helplessly, she watched it go. Faster and faster it rose until it was the size of a moon, then a star, and then there was nothing to see.

By the time Stephanie reached the camper she was hysterical, sobbing and calling for JD. Later she didn't remember how she'd awakened the people or what she'd said. She knew she was babbling. And she scared the life out of them. The man, pulling on his pants over long underwear, kept repeating, "What's she say? What's she talking about?" And his wife, holding Stephanie in her big warm arms right there at bedside in the camper, cradling and shushing and patting . . .

"What happened now? *Who* disappeared?" the woman asked when Stephanie finally quieted.

"We're camped down the road and we saw this . . . *thing!* But it's gone and I don't know where he is . . . my brother. He went out to take a picture of it."

"Was it a wild cat?" the man asked gruffly, at the same time lifting his rifle off the rack above the window.

"JD said it was a UFO. It was *huge*. And bright. Didn't you see anything?"

"A UFO?" the woman looked at her husband, then back at Stephanie. Quickly she pulled on a rough plaid coat and got her feet into some boots.

"Come on, Clarence, we'll have to drive up there."

Then they were all in the front seat of the camper truck, riding roughly along the same stretch of road Stephanie had just covered. They sat forward in their seats, scanning the road and the brush alongside wherever the lights touched. Then, as they came around the point of trees and into the clearing, the man slowed the truck, shining his brights on the VW with the driver's door still standing open, then on the lean-to with their rumpled sleeping bags inside.

"JD was running that way," Stephanie pointed toward the far line of trees, "when I last saw him." Her voice broke.

Clarence trained the truck lights on the middle of the clearing, then reached under the seat and handed his wife a flashlight.

"Take this, Ruth. I'll get the lantern."

Stephanie jumped down from the truck to get their own flashlight, then quickly hurried back to the camper.

"JD!" she called, "where are you? Can you hear me?" There was no answer.

"Jay Deeee," the others joined in. They stood listening. A bird fluttered somewhere behind them. Then silence again. Their lights showed nothing but the empty expanse of grass and sage.

"Fan out," Clarence instructed them. "We'll try to cover the clearing. And don't worry," he gripped Stephanie's arm. "See that streak of light over there? It'll soon be dawn. We'll find him."

At first every rock or stump picked up by her light was JD. Her heart leaped a dozen times. Then, scouring the far part of the clearing, she felt the panic return. Why didn't he answer? If he were there, he'd answer. If he hadn't been hurt . . . or worse. She kept calling his name, but her throat was so tight she hardly knew her own sounds. The possibility of never seeing him again was working at her, but she couldn't stop to think about it. Stumbling on, with more anxiety than she could handle, she almost missed the dark shape that caught on her light about fifty yards ahead. Instinctively, she stopped. She steadied the flashlight and brought it slowly back until she could make out a form on the ground. It had to be JD!

"He's here! Over here! I found him!" she called. Then she ran, choking back sobs of relief, saying mindless frantic prayers that he'd be all right. Soon she could see his orange parka and then the white of his hands and face. He was moving! He raised up, then lay back again.

"JD, are you all right?" she cried, inspecting him with her light, then kneeling to help him sit up. "What happened? I couldn't find you."

"I don't know," JD answered, sounding weak. He looked behind him. "It's gone." Then he turned to see the lights bobbing through the dark toward them. He grabbed Stephanie with hands as cold as ice. "Oh, God, they're coming!"

"It's okay, JD. It's the people in that camper, remember? They came to help find you."

"Oh," he moaned. He lay back and covered his face with both hands.

"Is he okay?" the woman asked as she came puffing up to them, closely followed by her husband.

"I don't know," Stephanie answered. "I think he's kind of stunned. Can you get up, JD?"

Together they helped him to his feet, then with Clarence and Stephanie steadying him on either side, they made their way back to the campsite. Almost there, JD began a violent shaking. "I'm freezing," he chattered. She could feel him shivering right through his parka.

Ruth hurried ahead. "You climb right on in," she said when they got to the camper. "It's nice and warm in there and Clarence can turn up the flame." She opened the door and held it for JD. Finally inside, she had him sit on the bed in front of the heater and pulled a blanket up to wrap around him.

"Thanks," JD smiled, looking especially pale by the overhead light, "I hate to bother you people."

"Bother?" she said in a stout voice. "Nonsense! Clarence

and I haven't had this much excitement in years!" Neither have we, Stephanie thought.

Ignoring JD, Ruth shed her jacket and wrapped herself in an old chenille robe. Her flannel pajamas still showed here and there, but it didn't seem to bother her.

Clarence joined them in the camper after checking around outside and quickly peeled off his coat. "Clarence Morris," he put out a big rough hand to JD. "I'm sure glad we found you. This young lady was just about beside herself."

JD tried to stand, but Mr. Morris gently pushed him back to the side of the bed.

"Did you . . . uh . . . did you folks see anything?" JD asked, still obviously shaken, as Clarence slid in behind the table.

"Nah. We were asleep. Then we heard all this racket—"

Ruth gave her husband a sharp look, heaping big spoons of coffee into a pot, "Without which you wouldn't have moved," she interrupted. "He sleeps like the dead!"

"Well, she got us up anyway," Clarence went on. "What happened? Your sister said you saw one of them flying saucers."

JD moved his hand over his face. "God," he looked around the camper as if searching for some way to explain it all. "I don't know how to tell you. Stephanie woke me up and this red light was all over everything . . . wasn't it?" he turned to his sister for confirmation.

"I thought it was the end of the world," she admitted sheepishly.

"It was bright as day," JD went on. "Then we saw this big thing, like a ball . . . a luminescent ball, sort of, just hanging over the power lines."

"I could see different colored lights on it later," Stephanie broke in.

"Then it landed in the clearing without making a sound," JD said. "It just kind of floated in."

"You mean to say it *landed?*" Clarence studied their faces.

"It must have. I grabbed my camera and got one shot standing behind the car. I didn't know what setting to use—it was so bright—so I opened her up about half." Suddenly JD turned to his sister. "Hey, did you pick up my camera?"

"No, I didn't see it," she answered.

"Don't fuss about it now," Ruth said, busy with a mixing bowl, "we'll go out and look after we have some coffee and pancakes. It's not going anywhere before daylight."

They all turned back to JD. "And then I started running . . ." JD looked confused. "I wanted to get closer, because I could see the lights were flashing on a kind of rim around the middle about then . . . but I can't remember if I got another picture . . ." he stopped talking. He frowned and looked at Stephanie, like maybe she could supply some answers.

"Did you fall? Were you knocked out? You were just lying out there, you know," Stephanie prodded.

"Steph, I don't know. I can't remember. I'm trying to put it all together . . ."

Stephanie felt a rush of sympathy for him. JD, with the super confidence, always on top. Wrapped in the blanket, his face white and drawn right now, he looked like someone else.

"You know," Clarence said, "there's been a lot of UFO talk around the Uintah Basin which isn't too far from here. But I always reckoned those Mormons were just seeing things," he laughed.

JD's eyes narrowed. "So help me, God, Mr. Morris, what we saw was real."

"Oh yeah. I can see you kids saw *something*," he agreed, smoothing it over. "I can see that!"

"When did it leave?" JD asked, turning back to his sister.

Then Stephanie told her side of the story, about the humming sound, the peculiar white color, finally the rapid rise and disappearance of the thing.

"And we slept through all that!" Ruth invited JD to the table and poured coffee for everyone. "It gives me the chills."

The pancakes Mrs. Morris scooped off the grill tasted awfully good to Stephanie, but she noticed JD didn't have much appetite. He drank his coffee, ate one pancake, then sort of seemed to drift into himself. Mostly *she* kept up the conversation with the Morrises, telling them where she and JD lived and how they were trying to get pictures of an elk herd for the *Times*. They were nice people, she decided. She could see they'd like to believe, even if they couldn't.

When the sky finally lightened enough for them to see their way around outside, Clarence got back into his coat and suggested they go "take a look-see." Ruth excused herself to get dressed, saying she'd be out with them in a minute, and JD swallowed the last of his coffee. He seemed to have forgotten their plans to seek out the big elk herd from some distant ridge. In Stephanie's mind, yesterday's simple pleasure in catching a family of elk going about their business seemed remote—like maybe a few light years remote. It didn't help, hunching against the biting, early morning wind, to see JD's shoulders drooping like an old man's, either.

The three of them crisscrossed the ground around the camp, but the camera was nowhere to be seen. Then Clarence and JD started out across the clearing. When Stephanie and Ruth finally caught up with the men, they found them staring in disbelief at the ground.

"God Almighty," Mr. Morris said softly under his breath. "God Almighty! This is right where she was!"

A large circle of scorched ground, maybe thirty feet across, enscribed as true as if by compass, lay before them.

"Don't step in there," JD warned Stephanie. "This whole place could be radioactive."

"It's been stirred up pretty good," Clarence said. "Some of the plants has been pulled right up by the roots."

"JD, I'm scared!"

"Now we've got to find that camera," JD turned to Stephanie. "With a picture of this someone might believe us. "Where . . . exactly . . ." he spread his arms to include the whole area, "was I when you found me?"

Stephanie shifted to get her bearings from the trees bordering the clearing. Then she looked back at the camper and sighted along a dead stump she had passed in the night.

"You were right . . . there," she pointed, not a stone's throw from the impression left by the strange night caller. The dirt, disturbed by several sets of footprints, bore her out.

THREE

By midmorning Mrs. Morris had tidied up the camper and was urging her husband to hurry.

"We're supposed to be at our daughter's tonight for dinner," she explained to Stephanie, "with two hundred miles to go. Will you and JD be all right if we leave?"

"Sure," Stephanie nodded, looking toward JD who seemed to be only half-listening to Mr. Morris' hunting story.

"C'mon, Clarence, they've got to break camp, too." Mrs. Morris shook her head. "He's a talker, ain't he?"

Finally, they all shook hands and said good-by, wishing one another a safe trip home.

"I'm gonna keep my eyes open," Clarence said from his window after climbing into the cab. "I might see one of them UFO's!" He treated them all to a hearty laugh as he waved and drove away.

In a few minutes Clarence Morris was pulling the camper onto the highway, heading back to Colorado. "Well, this'll be one to tell the neighbors about," he chuckled.

"I can't get over it," Ruth said, "those nice kids, scared to death, and out there all by themselves. I sure hope they get home all right."

"I suppose you swallowed all that about JD being her brother," Clarence suggested. "Guess I was born in the wrong generation. I'd never have dared take a girl out in the woods like that when I was young. Kids are brassy about it nowadays."

"Don't you think they were brother and sister?" Ruth acted surprised that he'd bring up such a thing.

"Nah, those two weren't a bit related."

"Clarence! I think you're wrong. They even looked alike. Except his hair was brown."

"You always think the best about people, Ruth, never question a thing. I suppose you believe they saw a real flying saucer, too, sportin' colored lights and zooming straight up in the sky?" he gestured.

"Well . . ." Ruth fumbled, "what do you think, if you know so much about it?"

"I think those two were on one helluva drug binge last night. Remember how peculiar that boy acted when we found him out there? And how wild she was here in the camper at first? They were seein' things all right!"

"But Clarence! That burned place in the grass. You said yourself that . . ."

"Well, I been thinking about that. There're at least a dozen ways kids could make a spot to look like that. Take a little charcoal starter fluid, for instance. Even lightning can tear up the ground and burn the vegetation. I've seen it myself. And he never found his camera," he added, "now did he?"

"I guess you think he never had one."

"Now you're talkin'! Never had a camera and never took pictures of the elk, either."

"I don't know, Clarence. They looked like they'd had some

terrible thing happen to them. Why would they tell us such a story and put on such a big act?"

"That's the only part I can't figure out," Clarence admitted.

Ruth looked away from her husband. For a long time she didn't say a word. Then, after inspecting the hands she held tightly clasped in her lap, she turned back to him. "They reminded me of Jim and Sally," she said.

Clarence put his big hand on his wife's knee and pulled her closer to him on the seat. "I could see that."

FOUR

"Let's go over it again," JD moved to make room for Stephanie on the log where he sat to rest. He lowered his head between his hands, pressing hard on his temples. The explosions of pain were hitting him rapid-fire now, but he hated to give in to it, just as he'd hated to give in to the vomiting that sent him into the brush after the Morrises left.

"Okay, JD," Stephanie sat down beside him. "We've covered every inch of ground eight times, but we'll do it again. Where should I start?"

"You know it couldn't disappear. All by itself, a camera doesn't just disappear."

"Maybe somebody took it. *They* took it. You know it's possible."

JD looked sideways at his sister. "You mean Clarence and Ruth?"

"No, I mean *they*. Whoever was in that UFO." She was serious, JD decided, not admitting he'd thought of it hours earlier.

"Oh, hell!" he swore and got to his feet. "Start here at camp. Go over the lean-to again, everything. Work your way out to me."

Stephanie walked toward the car with JD, her hands shoved in her pockets, scowling at the clearing and the trees beyond. "JD, how can this be happening to us?" She squinted up at him through the noon sunlight. "Can you believe what we saw last night. Really?"

"Of course I believe it. Don't you?"

"Yes, but it's so crazy! I don't understand it. I feel like somebody played a joke on us . . . a miserable, sick joke!"

"Stephanie, we both saw it. We couldn't be seeing identical illusions. Now could we?" His voice was impatient.

"No, but where'd it come from? What was that thing doing here? JD, it scares me. I'm afraid of what will happen to us."

"You mean," JD stopped, "maybe we saw something we shouldn't have—"

"Yes, and what if—"

"Steph, it's gone. You're not afraid right now, this minute, are you?"

She shook her head no, but her face continued to worry.

"Let's look for the camera once more, then I promise we'll pack up and head for home. You know how important it is to find the camera, don't you?"

She shook her head yes.

"Come on. We'll go together."

Stephanie tagged along with him, lifting each sage clump with a stick as they memorized again the texture of the clearing. He was actually glad for her company. It had been hard for them to talk in front of the Morrises, and then, afterward, he'd been so sick he'd only wanted to get off by himself. Once he got the nausea under control, he and Stephanie had searched everywhere—around the landing site, into the aspen on one side, and back to their camp on the other. They *had* covered everything eight times. But JD couldn't believe the camera wasn't still out there, somewhere, if they could just find it.

It was midafternoon by the time they finally broke camp. "The Morrises are probably home by now," Stephanie complained, jamming her things into the duffel bag. Finally, everything but the garbage was packed and ready to go.

"Aren't you going to eat your sandwich?" Stephanie asked JD who'd left his lunch untouched.

"I'm not hungry." He looked again over the matted grass where the lean-to had been, then circled around through the aspen and inspected the covered latrine. His last glance at the mountain took in the low-hanging cloud bank on the horizon.

"I guess we'd better get started. There's some weather moving in." JD pulled off his parka and threw it on the second seat of the car.

"Damn it, Stephanie!" He banged his fist down hard on top of the VW. "What could've happened to that camera?"

"Come on, JD. We've gotta go," Stephanie groaned.

"Yeah, we're going," his mouth was set in a hard line as he slid into the driver's seat. Then he held his breath until the engine caught, remembering what had happened with Stephanie. "Are you sure you tried the lights last night?" he asked.

"Double sure. And they didn't work either."

"I asked Clarence what might've happened to the car," JD said as they started down the road, tipsily swaying over the worst of the ruts.

"What'd he say?"

"He said you probably didn't know a key hole from a . . ." JD grinned but didn't finish the sentence.

"Oh, he did not!"

"Yes he did. And you know what? I could tell he didn't for a minute believe anything we told him. Unless it was out there where that thing landed."

"How's anyone going to believe us?" Stephanie asked. "Would you? I mean, if Chic told you he'd seen a big red UFO sitting out in a field, would you believe him?"

"I don't know," he answered. JD swung the car out on the state road and began the winding drive down Skull Mountain. Stephanie was probably right. Who'd believe them? He thought their folks would. He could hear his mother now, "If JD said it happened, it happened!" And Chic would try. He'd want to hear every detail about five times, then he'd go look it up in a book somewhere. In two weeks he'd be a UFO expert. But JD's list ended abruptly with those three.

Now he wished he'd eaten that sandwich. His head was still hurting and he felt dizzy, like he hadn't slept for a week. He ran his hand over his face, trying to wipe off the prickly feeling. It was the same on his hands, too, like a rash or an irritation. Nothing he could see, but a sensation, peculiar, like shivers on the skin.

"You know, Steph," he turned to his sister again, "the thing that nags me most is what happened after you left. It took you a while to bring the Morrises over to our camp. What was I doing all that time?"

Suddenly Stephanie's face brightened. "Hey. Remember when you fell off Petunia? You forgot everything. You didn't even know you'd been on a horse."

"Accident amnesia," JD labeled it for her. "But I didn't fall this time, that I know of."

"Maybe you just blacked out. You got too close and you blacked out. Maybe the UFO zapped you with a ray or something."

"Yeah, yeah," he said sarcastically, but he'd thought of that too.

"Can you remember taking another picture?"

"No. That's the funny part. I can't remember anything but running toward it. I could see the lights throbbing, from one side to the other, I think."

"Yeah, real fast. Then back again the other way."

"And I wanted to get a picture, but I kept on running. Like something just made me get closer and closer. God, Stephanie, I was so scared! But I couldn't stop."

"JD, that's awful! How did you stand it?"

"I guess I didn't."

"Carol Sue isn't going to believe one word of this!" Stephanie exclaimed. "But she'll be jealous it didn't happen to her anyway."

"Now wait a minute, Steph. You can't go blabbing all over."

"Carol Sue's my best friend. I'll have to tell *her*."

"But not the minute we get in the house. You know this story's going to make us look like a couple of loonies, don't you? I think I should talk to someone. Get some ideas. Heck, I don't even know what happened myself."

"*Who?* Just who would you talk to?"

"Well, I was thinking of Garth."

"What could *he* say?"

"I don't know. But he's been around. He's twice our age. He might know if we should report it to someone or just keep our mouths shut."

At the foot of the mountain the road straightened out and widened to a normal two lane. JD was glad for the easier driving. He decided to stop for a hamburger as they entered the only town between Skull Mountain and Red Butte. Maybe eating something would help.

"Want some fries and a Coke?" he asked. Stephanie's face lit up. He was glad she was easy to please. He didn't have much money.

It was getting dark when they finally pulled into Red Butte. They'd managed to keep ahead of the storm front, but the sky looked like it might unload any minute. Since their parents were usually at the laundromat until eight, JD would have time to unpack and see Garth first. He made Stephanie promise not to say anything until he returned, then headed across town in his VW.

Garth Magleby, JD's tenth grade history teacher and now the high school counselor, was one of the few people JD could trust with such a far-out story. Besides, he was almost one of the family. Garth had gone fishing with him and his dad more times than he could count.

"Where we fishing tomorrow, John?" he'd call through the Anderson's screen door on a Saturday night. His dad would get up to let him in, looking pleased but sounding mad. "Hell, Magleby, you're getting to be a regular pest. Can't you find anyone else to fish with? Jeezus Christ in a wheelbarrow!"

With everyone laughing then, Garth would march right into the kitchen, pour himself a mug of coffee, and they'd begin to plan. The three of them would be out on the stream by six o'clock the next morning. It was always a strain to call his fishing buddy "Mr. Magleby" Monday mornings at school, but JD hadn't slipped yet.

Now, striding across the browned lawn to the little frame house where Garth lived alone, JD turned scared. He hoped he wouldn't make an ass of himself. How was he going to tell Garth, anyway?

"Hey, look who's here," Garth met him at the door wearing blue jeans and a sheepskin vest. Garth's close-trimmed red beard surrounded the friendliest smile JD had seen all weekend. "Come on in, JD!" he threw open the door. "What's it going to do, rain or snow?"

JD felt better already. "Both," he said.

"Here, take off your coat. You got an elk report for me?"

"We saw three. And some deer from a distance. Mostly it was quiet." *Quiet!* The word made faces at him.

"That doesn't sound so good. Maybe we'll have to hunt up in the timber." Garth pulled out a chair for JD. "You better sit a spell."

"The snow might bring 'em down," JD stalled, thinking maybe he wouldn't say anything to Garth after all about the UFO. It was comfortable enough just sitting there at the dining room table where they always talked. Actually he'd never *seen* the table in its entirety. Tonight, as usual, it was covered with papers—aptitude tests, merit-test folders, pamphlets, fish and game bulletins, paperback books on geology and cross-country skiing and fly-tying.

"Can I get you a Coke?" Garth offered. "You want one of Kay Eagleton's cinnamon rolls? She thinks I'm losing weight," he chuckled. "If I look haggard enough when I'm over there she bakes me something."

"No. No, thanks," JD said.

There was a long silence, then Garth leaned forward and studied JD's face at close range.

"No Coke? You're sick," he announced.

It was the opening JD was waiting for. "Maybe I am," he began, shifting uneasily in the chair.

"What's wrong?" Garth frowned. When his face took on the serious counselor look, JD knew he was committed. After stumbling for a beginning, he finally just said it, straight out. "Stephanie and I saw a UFO up there, and it scared the daylights out of us."

Then JD told him everything, about the strange force that drew him to the craft—or whatever it was—about the amnesia, about Stephanie's watching it take off. Finally, he threw in the unbelievable disappearance of the camera. They talked for a long time, Garth asking the same questions JD had been asking himself all day.

"Seeing something like that in the middle of the night would scare the hell out of anybody," Garth said, scratching his head and stretching out in his chair, "but tell me this. Have you noticed anything unusual since then? Any physical symptoms, for instance?"

"My head hasn't stopped hurting and I threw up earlier today. I don't know if there's a connection or not. But the funniest thing is my skin. On my hands and face . . ."

"What about it?"

"It prickles or . . . tingles. It's hard to describe. Like maybe using rubbing alcohol. You know?"

"Hmmm. Did you get sunburned?"

"Some, maybe. But this feels different. It's weird."

Garth's eyes narrowed. He was trying to find some logic in JD's story. "What do you think happened, JD? During the time you were left alone? Why'd you pass out?"

"I've tried and tried to remember," JD frowned, biting at his lower lip. He leaned forward, gesturing toward the street. "I got maybe as close as my car out there. And I ducked down low to try for another picture . . ."

Suddenly JD felt very uncomfortable. He wanted to get out

of there—to run somewhere. He gripped the arms of his chair and his breathing came fast just as it had before. The heat of nausea rose again in his throat.

"Take it easy, JD. It's okay," Garth reached for him.

"No . . . no!" JD said, looking through Garth, seeing something else. He started perspiring. "Garth! God! I was . . . I was *in* it . . . inside that thing!"

"What do you mean?" Garth jumped to his feet.

"I couldn't remember anything before. It was a blank. Just now, like a flash, I saw the inside of that UFO! I was *in* there! God, what happened to me?"

"Hold on, JD. You're under a lot of stress. Are you *sure* you really saw something?"

JD held his head between his hands, pressing, pressing, to ease the pain. He didn't *want* to know, he didn't *want* to see *anything*.

"Are you all right?" Garth knelt beside him.

JD caught his breath again. He swallowed the welling sickness in his throat. "I don't know," he moaned. "Garth, I thought I was going to die."

FIVE

Perched on the tall kitchen stool, Stephanie held the phone in one hand and brushed her hair full length with the other. It was never easy to break away from Carol Dougan.

"I still have to wash my hair and do some math," she twisted around to check the clock above her head. "No, I'll tell you more about it later. JD made me promise."

Stephanie held on for another minute of listening. Carol Sue was never going to quit. She'd saved it up all weekend and had to get everything in right now.

"Look, Dougan, I have to go," Stephanie slid off the stool. "I'm going to hang up now . . ." It was her last resort. " 'Bye."

Now she'd really have to hustle. She liked to wash her hair in their deep, old-fashioned kitchen sink, but if she didn't hurry everyone would be home and she'd still be dripping. She closed the kitchen curtains and took off her shirt. Then, just as she was working up a good lather, she heard her mother's steps on the front porch and knew she shouldn't have stayed on the phone so long.

"Well, hi there, Dumplin's!" her mom said, coming in.

She set a grocery sack on the counter and took off her coat. "I didn't think you were home yet."

"Hi," Stephanie managed an upside down smile from the depths of the sink.

"Where's JD?"

"He went to Garth's. He said he'd be home by eight."

"Now, why's he bothering Garth on a Sunday night?"

Stephanie ran her rinse water, glad she didn't have to answer.

"Did you have a good time?" her mother asked, tying on an apron.

"Uh huh."

"You didn't freeze Saturday night? It went down to thirty-five here."

"Nope."

"Did JD see any elk?" Her mom went right on, seasoning the pork chops and bustling around.

"Mom, wait, I can't talk." The water made rivers to her mouth and eyes both. She wished JD would hurry. She wasn't very good at holding back from her mother who always liked to hear everything.

Back in her denim shirt once again, wearing the towel like a turban, Stephanie sat down at the table and watched her mother cut up potatoes for hash browns. Stephanie was glad to be home. Here she felt a hundred per cent safe. The hot chops frying and the coffee perking spelled pure comfort after three days of camping.

"Where's Dad?" Stephanie asked, thinking to steer the conversation another way.

"He'll be along. Mrs. Carlin was still folding a load."

"What did you guys do while we were gone?"

Her mother looked surprised that she would ask. "We

worked. I went to church this morning. Dad fooled around with the pickup and finally got it running. He thinks we need a new fuel pump." She walked to the stove and dumped the potatoes into the hot skillet.

Stephanie wished her mother had an easier life—or maybe a more glamorous life, she wasn't sure which. When *she* got to be fifty, she hoped she'd still have a waistline that showed, anyhow, and a hair-do that looked modern. Kay Eagleton was only ten years younger than her mother, but they looked a generation apart. Ranch life was hard on a woman, Stephanie supposed.

"You haven't told me a thing," Addie Anderson came back to the table with a stack of plates. "I suppose Garth gets to hear about your trip before I do." Her blue eyes turned snappy. "Some big deal being the mother, huh?"

"Mom . . ." Stephanie looked down at her hands. "JD made me promise to save the . . . exciting part for after he got home." She felt her cheeks flush.

Her mother stopped what she was doing, a plate still in her hand.

"What happened? Is JD hurt? Did you wreck the car?"

"No, nothing like that." Stephanie walked to the window and opened the curtains to look out. It had started to rain.

"Stephanie, something *did* happen. Why can't you tell me?"

When Stephanie turned back, the look of worry on her mother's face reflected all they'd been through, she and JD, in the last eighteen hours. I can't keep it from her, Stephanie thought, fighting the fears that washed over her again, as fresh as running down the mountain road for help. Suddenly Stephanie's face contorted.

"Oh, Mom," she blurted out, "it was terrible!"

She rushed to her mother and threw her arms around her, burying her face in Addie's neck. "I was so scared!" she sobbed.

"Oh, baby, baby, what happened to you?"

SIX

Garth had never seen JD in such a state before. Here was a solid, stable kid, not given to hallucinations or trumped-up stories. Then what in the hell was going on? JD had been terrified. By a UFO, he'd said. Worse, he now had the notion that he'd been *inside* it. It was too unlikely for Garth. But how could he account for JD going to pieces the way he did?

They had sat at the table another hour, going over everything again, trying to find plausible explanations.

"I think you should report it," Garth said when JD finally stood to leave. Garth hitched his thumbs in his belt and studied the floor, thinking. "The Air Force used to collect data, but they don't anymore. Maybe a local report, here in Red Butte, to the police . . ."

"They'd laugh their heads off," JD said. He looked discouraged enough as it was.

"Maybe not. If someone else saw something and reported it, confirming your sighting, you know, it would give you some peace of mind."

"What would I . . . how would I go about it?"

Garth ran his hand over his beard and ended up stroking his sideburns. He looked pretty grubby to be calling on Mike

Butzow the way he was, but he wondered if JD should wait. "I don't think you should put it off. Do you want me to go with you . . . right now? You'll feel better."

"Yeah, would you?" JD looked relieved.

"Let me grab my coat and make a phone call. Kay was expecting me to come over."

"No, wait, Garth, I don't have to do this tonight."

"No sweat. I'll just tell her I can't make it. I'll explain later."

It was raining by the time JD pulled up to the squat brick building on the outskirts of town. The two windows flanking the door read State Highway Patrol on one side and Red Butte Police on the other. Garth always wondered if they were compatible. Tonight the Highway Patrol office was closed, but Mike Butzow sat at the typewriter on the police side filling out some kind of form. Lenny Jones, the county deputy sheriff, was leafing through a *Field and Stream* at a table farther back.

Mike recognized them both as they came in. "Hi there, Magleby," he went right on pecking at the keys, "you making a citizen's arrest on this boy?"

"Me?" JD grinned.

"I've seen you pushing thirty-five on Center Street in that yellow Volkswagen," he waggled a finger at JD as he swiveled to face them. "Your ticket's made out, you know. All's I have to do is put the right date on it."

We'll be lucky to get a word in, Garth thought.

"What can I do you for?" Mike lifted his heavy body out of the chair with some effort and came up to the counter. JD looked at Garth. Plainly, he didn't know how to start. Garth began for him.

"JD and his sister just got back from the Gorge this afternoon, Mike. He was trying to get a picture of the elk herd they say is up there—Crawford promised to run it in the *Times*."

"Oh, yeah?" Mike was looking interested. "Did you see any?"

"Only three. No big herds."

"But wait'll you hear what they *did* see," Garth opened the way for JD. "Go ahead. You tell him."

JD's face reddened. Clearly, he wasn't going to enjoy this. "Well," he began, "we saw something we couldn't identify. I guess it was a UFO. And we thought . . . Garth here, thought, that we oughta report it."

"A UFO!" Officer Butzow leveled his eyes on JD. He wasn't smiling. "Lenny, you better come up and hear this."

"It was Saturday night—or this morning rather, maybe three or four o'clock," JD went on. "And we don't know how long it had been there, but the light woke up Stephanie and she started shaking me. In the lean-to, you know."

Then JD made the full report, with occasional grunts and "what do you know's" coming from Mike and a steady background smirk from Lenny. Garth was relieved to see he'd left out the suggestion that he'd been inside the UFO. When he had finished, Mike urged JD to take his story to Mr. Crawford at the *Times* as well.

"There was a report—middle of last week," Mike said, "that came into Cheyenne from a tourist couple. They were down in the Utah Canyonlands and said they'd been followed in their car by a big orange light that started and stopped when they did. The papers down there said it was Venus. This guy got mad as hell when he read it, so he reported the whole story again in Cheyenne."

"Is that right?" Garth shook his head.

"The officer over here," Mike nodded toward the highway patrol sector, "was followed once himself in the middle of the night. Just last fall when the Uintah Basin was thick with them."

The deputy sheriff wasn't saying anything.

"'Course, Lenny, here, he don't believe in UFO's," Mike said.

"Neither did I," JD shoved his hands in his pockets and shifted his weight, looking uneasy, "but I do now. I tell you, I do now!"

Then Mike produced a clipboard and some paper. "Sit down over there, JD." He pointed to a school-type desk under the "Wanted" posters. "Let's have you write it out. Just the bare bones of it. But give the place and time as best you can and some detail in the description. Write what your sister saw that you didn't, and we won't have to bother her."

JD raised his eyebrows at Garth with an expression that said, "Look what you got me into." Garth shrugged and smiled, mostly because he couldn't help himself. JD needed a shave and his eyes looked like two pee holes in a snowbank. He'd think twice before he saw another flying saucer.

It was pouring down rain when they left the police station in JD's car. Garth asked JD if he could stand to tell his story one more time. "Crawford will put it in the paper, that's for sure. He's so short of news he prints funeral sermons just to fill space."

"Yeah, but maybe I don't want to go on record to the whole town."

"Why not?"

"Hell, Garth, everyone will think I'm some kind of weirdo."

"Suit yourself. You'll have to tell Crawford what happened

to the camera, won't you? I don't think you should be afraid of the publicity, JD. These folks in Red Butte know you."

Why am I trying to talk him into it? Garth thought, letting the regular beat of the windshield wiper mesmerize him. He tried to remember what it was like being seventeen, if he'd have done any better than JD—stammering around, trying to convince someone that the impossible had just happened. Garth was ready to suggest that they go on home when JD spoke up ahead of him.

"Okay. I'll do it. If one other person saw that UFO, you know, along the highway someplace . . . maybe printing our story would bring theirs out."

"Right," Garth said with more enthusiasm than he actually felt. "Someone has to be first. I sure wish I'd been there with you, JD. I'd like to see that circle where you say it landed."

"Could we get back up there before everything's snowed in?" JD suggested. "Would you want to go?"

Garth hated to squelch JD's hopes, but the rain they were having was probably the snow base for sixty inches that would accumulate on the mountains this winter. Garth squinted out of the windshield. "It's snowing up there now, I'd say, and likely won't melt off 'til spring."

It was Mrs. Crawford who came to the door and asked them in, waiting politely while they wiped their feet on the mat a decent number of times. Mae Crawford had been Garth's principal at the old Red Butte High School, and he admitted she still had a formidable presence.

"He's relaxing with the ten o'clock news," she said with a tight smile, "but I'll tell him you're here. Please sit down."

They stood just inside the french doors of what might have been an elegant parlor at one time. Finally, they heard footsteps coming from the back of the big house. Tom Crawford, his bony frame showing through an old sweater, came into the room with about twice the cordiality his wife had mustered. "Well, well, hello there," he shooks hands with Garth and gestured the two to sit down. "Imagine having company on a blustery night like this." He looked pleased, Garth thought, to have his relaxing interrupted. Crawford was a canny old bastard, carrying on with the *Times* long after most small town papers had gone under. Garth respected him. And Red Butte supported him, even though they bought his paper purely out of habit and curiosity. Their neighbors' doings were of more importance to this ranch community than the national crises Crawford was inclined to ignore.

"Hope you're not bringing bad news," the older man said, taking in the situation. "I enjoy a social call. Folks don't drop in like they ought to."

JD cleared his throat and looked across the room at Garth. Garth made no move to come to his rescue this time.

"You see, I don't have any pictures of the elk herd for you, Mr. Crawford. I guess that's bad news," JD smiled weakly, "for me, anyhow."

"No picture! Well, well, well. Why not?" He reached for a box of cigars on the end table and offered them around.

"I did get some beautiful shots, close up, too, of a cow and bull elk and a calf watering at the beaver dam," JD's eyes brightened. "Mr. Crawford, it was like a still life. They just stood there looking at me. I got maybe three, four frames before they moved."

"Sounds good enough," Crawford said, working at his cigar. "Come into the office and we'll develop 'em tomorrow."

"That's the trouble. I lost the camera." Then JD launched into his story from the beginning.

The smoke from Mr. Crawford's stogies hung in multiple layers by the time they stood to leave his parlor. He'd been especially keen to hear JD's description of the UFO—the sound it made, the angle of flight, the position of the lights around the central rim. It seemed that Crawford had read a great deal about UFO's. His library included some of the earliest books about the strange craft that began appearing in numbers after 1947 all over the world.

"I can't say I'm a believer," he confessed after hearing JD's story, "but I'm not a complete skeptic either. A lot of reliable people—including you, JD—have seen things they can't explain."

He walked across the room and opened a desk. "Ever see a copy of *Flying Saucer Review?* It's the only one I have, but you're welcome to borrow it."

Mr. Crawford put his hand on JD's shoulder as he walked them back into the vestibule. "Why don't you write up your UFO sighting and we'll run it this Wednesday? Tell your sister to add her side of it, and I'll edit the whole shebang so it fits together."

JD thanked Mr. Crawford for seeing them at such a late hour—the hall clock now stood at eleven-thirty. Then Garth asked him to give their apologies to his wife, Mae.

"Sure thing," Tom waved at the door. "I enjoyed the visit."

Garth believed he had. The thing he himself dreaded most about getting old was the stillness, the oppressive quiet that attended nursing homes and old people's lives. They'd for sure disturbed Tom Crawford's quiet tonight. And he looked livelier for it, Garth decided. He waved again at the skinny old man silhouetted in the circle of light on the front porch.

SEVEN

The yellow VW entered the school parking lot just as the warning bell sounded. It was bad enough to get a late start on a day when he had so much on his mind, JD was thinking. He'd felt sick at breakfast, then to make matters worse, he'd got behind slow-moving traffic on Center Street. No one was ever ready for the first heavy snowfall that invariably hit the town overnight. Now, late to school and with only four hours of sleep, he remembered that Gayle would be waiting for him at his locker.

He said good-by to Stephanie who, still conscientious as a sophomore, slogged off across the snow-covered parking lot well ahead of her brother. JD gathered up his books and lunch, double-checked to see that his lights were off, then locked the car. He wanted to see Gayle this morning. Usually she'd wait, even if she didn't make first period on time. He hurried to join the dwindling group of bus students entering the side door of the building.

Down one corridor and to the left. He tried to suck in the smile on his face. Cool it, he told himself. You're always too eager. Then he saw her, looking a little put-out, but still waiting. There were other cute girls in school, but no one like

Gayle in JD's opinion. She was beautiful, a kitten and a bitch, with emerald-green eyes and soft brown hair that always smelled of shampoo. She also had about a thousand other qualities that appealed to him. She knew he adored her. Sometimes that in itself was a problem.

"You're late!" she scolded as he slipped his free arm around her waist and rubbed his cheek on top of her head.

"Yeah, I know," he nuzzled down to her mouth and was rewarded with a kiss that matched his own.

"Not now," she gently pushed him away, teasing with her enormous eyes. "Do you have to work after school?"

He sighed as he threw his books in the locker. "Yeah. Simon Legree has me down for two weeks solid."

"You're impossible!" she complained, leaning against the lockers. "Did you miss me?"

"What do you think?" He drew her close again. But it wasn't Gayle he saw when he closed his eyes for another kiss. It was a glowing ball of orange light shimmering above the power lines on Skull Mountain. The second bell rang.

"Walk me to class, JD," she begged, taking his hand and tugging him playfully along after her. "Daddy says you can't come over nights after work anymore, except weekends. How are we ever going to see each other?"

They had nearly reached her English class. She pulled her face into a sad pout and JD took her chin in his hand. "We'll think of something," he whispered. "Meet you for lunch."

He wasn't worried. Her dad had issued about thirty ultimatums so far this year, but Gayle always got around them some way. He, too, wished that he didn't have to put in so many hours working, but he didn't have a choice. He wanted to go to college. Besides, Gayle wouldn't look at him twice if he didn't. She was from that kind of family. They liked degrees and respectability and money.

JD hardly heard the chemistry lecture that day. Safely hidden in the fifth row of the class, he began to write his account of the UFO sighting. He felt a little easier this morning about having it in the paper than he had the night before. He'd read the *Flying Saucer Review* until 2:00 A.M. He couldn't put it down. Stranger experiences than Stephanie's and his—from France, Venezuela, Germany, the United States—were reported there in detail. A week ago he would have laughed at every one of them.

The bell rang, but JD, still writing, didn't move.

"Hmmm. Such copious notes! Did I say all that in one hour?" It was JD's chemistry teacher standing right at his elbow and his tone was unmistakably sarcastic. Everyone else had left the room. Embarrassed to be caught, JD snapped shut his notebook and smiled feebly.

"Well, I . . ." he couldn't think of a thing to say.

"Pay attention tomorrow," Mr. Grosbeck said and walked out into the hall.

JD would have liked to discuss the charred circle of ground with someone who knew chemistry like Grosbeck, but he knew he wouldn't. No one ever dropped in at room 204 uninvited. "*Gross* Beck," they called him behind his back.

By the time JD met Gayle at the east door, the one exit where they could sneak out to the parking lot for lunch, he had decided not to tell her anything about the UFO. Not yet. Maybe tonight or tomorrow night—after work.

They didn't open their lunches until they'd restored and nourished themselves with a long embrace and a dozen kisses.

"Who needs to eat?" JD whispered at Gayle's ear.

"Ummm, not me," she snuggled closer. "It was a long weekend."

"Bet you didn't think of me once," he teased, privately acknowledging his own guilt.

"Twice!" she laughed, pulling away and reaching to the back seat for their paper sacks. "Friday night when mother and I ate at the Inn," she opened her own lunch and retrieved an apple, "and Saturday when I bought a new outfit. Two times! Not bad, huh?"

"Wow, I'm overwhelmed!"

"Did you and Wilcox find the elk herd?"

"Chic couldn't go. I took Stephanie." JD started on his ham sandwich.

"Really? She went with you? I bet that was kind of an ordeal for her."

JD didn't answer.

"What'd you guys do all that time? Just run around looking for elk? Sounds awful!"

"Well . . ." JD frowned. "We got some pictures . . . sort of." What could he say? "The mountains are great this time of year, Gayle," he pushed on with it, trying to sound enthusiastic. "Someday I want to take you up there."

"Thanks anyway!" she wrinkled her nose in distaste. "Hey, did I tell you we're going to Phoenix at Christmas?"

"You said you might."

"Dad's decided for sure. We've written our cousins and everything."

JD was glad to be talking about *her* plans, relieved that it didn't take much encouragement to keep her on the subject. By the time they finished eating it was one o'clock, cause for a quick scramble to sort out their books. Then, hand in hand, leaping across the snow, they ran back to the building. JD congratulated himself. It wasn't always this easy to keep something from Gayle.

The last class of the day was the one JD lived for, and if the school paper was any good at all, he liked to think it was because he cracked the whip as front-page editor and opinion columnist. The kids in Journalism II were his closest friends at school. With only ten of them on the staff, they were a tight and loyal group. Their advisor, Miss McGinnis, had another class that hour so they succeeded or failed pretty much on their own. She red-penciled their mild insurrections, corrected their sentence structure, and set the deadlines; otherwise, she trusted them to get out *The Renegade* themselves.

Today they were beginning a new issue. JD got to the staff room early to chalk up their assignment columns on the blackboard. There was a certain excitement about the open, waiting space. Maybe this would be the issue to immortalize *The Renegade*. There was always that sweet possibility, anyway.

Chic Wilcox was the first one to arrive. JD was glad. He'd looked for a chance to see him all day. They exchanged a few blows, Chic ducking behind his glasses to exaggerate his vulnerability.

"How come you pick on me?" Chic whined in his weakling imitation. He looked the part, so skinny his chest was concave. But the wiry bright-eyed Wilcox kid, admittedly the class comic, was also well on his way to being class valedictorian. He laughed at himself *first*, and the other kids loved it. Among Chic's friends, only Gayle hadn't warmed to him, but JD thought she might be jealous. He and Chic had always bummed around together.

"Take seats, take seats," Chic stood at the door acting in

his own official capacity. "Take seats, everyone. Board of Directors meeting today. Did you bring your brains, Fatso?" he asked a ninety-eight pound girl who tweaked his cheek as she came into the room. "Harry Bean," he called down the hall, "this is your cubicle. Right this way."

JD shook his head and laughed. Chic would have them all organized and geared for work by the time the bell rang.

Then Fred Tomlin walked in and made his earth shattering announcement. JD, still at the blackboard at the back of the room, stopped writing in midsentence.

"See any UFO's lately?" Fred paused for effect. "I heard our honorable editor spent his weekend at the Gorge with an Un-ident-i-fied Fly-ing Ob-ject," he drew it out.

"You calling Stephanie names?" Chic danced into the room like a featherweight pugilist, his fists punching the air.

"Where'd you hear that?" JD turned around. Everyone was listening now. Even Chic stopped at the tone of his voice.

"C'mon, who told you that?" JD asked again.

"At lunch. The guys at our table said you made a police report last night."

Mike Butzow, JD thought, or Lenny. Man, you couldn't keep a secret in this crummy town.

Chic sidled up to JD. "What's he talking about?" The others left their seats and pulled up on desk tops at the back of the room, surrounding JD.

"Did you really see a UFO?" a girl asked.

"Hey, what happened?"

"What'd you hear, Fred?"

"Let *him* tell it," Fred looked rebuffed. "I wasn't there."

JD didn't know what to do. He hated being put on the spot.

"Look, you guys, we've got a paper to make up. Let's get

the assignments passed out, and we can talk later," his voice was all business, but his suggestion met with a stiff silence. A couple of the kids exchanged looks. Chic folded his arms, put that "make me" expression on his face, and plunked himself solid as a sphinx right under JD's nose. No one said a word. JD got the message in a hurry.

"Okay," he shrugged. He carefully set the chalk and eraser back on the chalk tray and slid up on a corner of the work table. "Shut the door, Claudia," he nodded at one of the girls. "Are we all here?" He took a quick head check and decided no one else would be coming in.

As it turned out, they didn't make up the paper that day. They did decide JD should do a feature on his UFO sighting and that Elaine Caldwell would interview Stephanie for the new issue. Then Chic got into a loud argument with the staff photographer on propulsion and fuels. In spite of the bedlam in the room after JD finished telling them, he felt relieved. True, his headache was back and going over it again caused the funny prickling on his hands and face to return, but he thought they'd believed him. Most of them. Of course, Fred had to bring up little green men with claw hands and pointy ears. There was a fair share of shrieking and giggling and a whole lot of speculation. But it was Chic who posed the question that bothered him the most.

"What if they brain-washed you some way to make you forget? Would you be able to bring it all back under hypnosis?" JD hadn't thought of that.

"Maybe I ought to probe your subconscious . . ." Chic's smile turned malicious.

"Forget it!"

"Seriously. You saw me put those kids under in health class . . ."

"And at Helen Leonard's, yeah, I remember. You're fantastic, Chic, but skip it, will you?"

After the bell Chic waited and walked with JD to his locker. His curiosity was still fired up.

"Did you feel any different?" he persisted. "After you came to?"

"I felt rotten. I still have a headache off and on that's a real bitch." He didn't mention the sensation on his skin or the nausea yesterday.

"I'll tell you what I think," Chic looked at his watch. "I gotta go to work, but I'll tell you what I think . . ." he paused.

"Spit it out," JD said. Sometimes Chic got so busy thinking, he'd forget what he was saying.

"That UFO confiscated your camera. They're passing your pictures around in some other galaxy right now."

JD had to laugh.

"Keep loose," Chic called as he hurried off down the hall.

On his way out of the building, JD stuck his head in at Garth's office. "How you doing?"

Garth waved, but didn't get up from his desk. "I'm zonked. How about you?"

"Likewise," JD grinned and moved out with the crowd.

Half an hour later, after taking Stephanie home and grabbing milk and a peanut butter sandwich, JD signed in at the Holiday Inn Restaurant just off the freeway outside town. He hated his job, but it had been the only one available. His boss, a tall, cranky penny-pincher named Bob Gillispie, had hinted that he might get promoted to maintenance if he "worked out" in the dining room. He guessed he'd be on probation forever because he was still clearing tables after six

68

months on the job. Now, shortly before they opened for the dinner trade, he had plenty to do.

JD got into a clean blue jacket that the kitchen boys wore and went on into the dining room to check the waitress' station for ice and serving utensils. Sylvie threw him a smile across the room where she was setting tables. She bent toward him, sweeping across the table to straighten the cloth, presumably treating him to a bird's eye view of her cleavage. She's always throwing it around, JD smiled in spite of himself. He wondered why she didn't put more of a premium on what she had.

Mr. Gillispie came into the room before they had any chance at conversation. He grunted, straightened a fork, nodded at JD and left again. Sylvie made a face at his back and motioned for JD to come over.

"Is it true, what I heard about you today?" she asked, batting her false eyelashes at him.

"What'd you hear?" He was expecting one of her dirty jokes. She heard and overheard more conversations than the C.I.A. But in spite of her "frippery," as his mother called it, Sylvie was everybody's favorite. She had a way with kids and little old ladies. Even men known to be light tippers left bills under their plates for Sylvie. She edged close to him.

"I heard you went out star gazing and got your eyes full."

"Shit!" JD said under his breath. He turned on his heel and stalked out of the room. It was all over town. Who needed to put anything in the papers in this place? He could hear Sylvie laughing all the way back to the kitchen.

EIGHT

Stephanie woke up Saturday morning wishing she hadn't. She rolled back into her pillow, deciding she'd rather be late for work than feel the cold linoleum on her bare feet right then. Why was she so tired? she wondered. Carol Sue hadn't left until midnight, then just as she'd dozed off, JD came in, banging around his room and running the shower. Sometime later she was awake again when JD had moaned and cried out in his sleep. Now, Stephanie was suddenly wide awake. She sat up on the edge of the bed and reached for her robe. What was it JD had said? "Get away. Get away from me!" And then he'd trailed into a long series of "No, no, no's" that seemed to end the nightmare. A short time later he was at it again, mostly babbling so she couldn't understand what he said. Finally, she'd called to him and he quit. He'd talked in his sleep Wednesday night, too, but she hadn't said anything about it.

Now Stephanie quietly left her room, glanced across the hall at JD's bedroom, then tiptoed down the stairs to the kitchen. John David, Sr., also in robe and pajamas, was working over the coffee pot.

71

"Gonna have breakfast with your old dad?" he asked without turning around. "I've got biscuits going."

"Already?" she crossed the room to where he stood at the stove and gave him a bear hug from behind. He patted her arm.

"I couldn't sleep," he said. "What time did JD get in?"

"Late. He worked until eleven. He probably stopped off at Gayle's afterward." I could do without biscuits this morning, she was thinking, but her dad loved them heaped with butter and plum jelly. It was what he'd grown up on, he always said. She wondered if she'd be telling her kids the same thing about Sugar Puffs and Corn Flakes. She opened a can of juice and set the table for two, placing her dad's medicine beside his plate. She hadn't heard him cough so much this morning. Maybe the new pills were doing some good.

"Want an egg?" her father asked, cracking one for himself into the frying pan.

"I guess," Stephanie couldn't stop yawning.

"What was JD hollering about in the night?"

"Did he wake you up, too?"

"A couple of times. He's been dreaming about that UFO, I suppose. I don't know what we're going to do with him."

"Dad," Stephanie had said it before. "I wish it had happened to you. If you'd seen that thing in the middle of the night, you'd be having nightmares, too. It was awful!"

"Sure, honey, I know. That's why I'm worried about JD. He's not eating so good. And all those phone calls since it came out in the *Times*. He didn't do any school work all week that I could see."

Stephanie held up her plate for the egg and some biscuits.

"If it just sort of . . . dies down, he'll be okay. Don't you think?" Her dad didn't need anything more to worry about.

"I hope so. People around here are so damned curious. They won't let him be." He poured steaming cups for both of them.

It was nice to be having coffee alone with her dad. It happened so seldom. They stirred in their cream and sugar, then talked about the article in the paper and what people had said about it at the laundromat. "Well, it brought in more business," her father said, smoothing the wispy gray hairs that stood up on top of his head, "but that's all the good it's done."

"It's all anybody wants to talk about at school," Stephanie sighed. "The UFO. Did we or didn't we really see one? So I just let 'em rattle on."

Stephanie finished her coffee then stood to go get dressed. "See you at dinner, Pops," she said, kissing him on the cheek. "Tell Mom I'll be home around four."

Stephanie knew she was lucky to work for Kay Eagleton. There weren't enough jobs in Red Butte to go around. You had to be sixteen to clerk in the dime store or at Geyerman's Ready-to-Wear, and her mother wouldn't let her apply at the A and W because of the late hours. Also, Mrs. Eagleton had promised to use Stephanie at Kay's Korners, her book and stationery shop, during the Christmas season. Stephanie knew she'd love that.

As it was, Kay Eagleton's house was so clean, Stephanie felt like she hardly earned her pay. She'd have the dusting, vacuuming and scrubbing finished by noon. In the afternoon she'd do some baking. If she finished early, which she always did, she'd read some of Kay's magazines or go in the bathroom and smell her cosmetics. Sometimes Kay asked her to do some touch-up ironing. That was her favorite job. The

73

blouses and knit pantsuits were pure luxury, always expensive and always smelling faintly of the natural earth scents Kay liked.

That Saturday afternoon Stephanie decided to bake the packaged devil's food cake she found in the cupboard. She was just swirling the buttery smooth frosting around the sides when Kay came home.

"Ooh, what's for dessert?" Mrs. Eagleton called from the front door. "Smells delicious."

She entered the kitchen still unbuttoning her leather coat (from Neiman Marcus, the label said) and engulfed Stephanie in her arms.

"Cinderella!" she smiled, rapturously, "you've done it again."

Stephanie laughed. It was so easy to please Kay. Whatever she made in the kitchen, Kay thought it was the greatest.

"This is the happiest part of Saturday, to come home to find you here." She ran a finger along the edge of the cake plate. "Hmmm. Marvelous!"

"JD says I'll never learn to cook—"

Kay wrinkled her nose in protest. "Your mother's spoiled him. He just won't admit to your great talents."

Stephanie finished frosting the cake while Kay took off her coat and checked the mail. "Now don't say a word," she came back into the kitchen, "because right now we're going to cut into this creation and have a piece together."

"Oh, do you really want to?" Stephanie usually left as soon as Kay got home.

"Yes, really," she smiled again. "For two reasons," Kay sliced down through the layers. "First, we never take time to talk. And we should, with no children of my own . . . milk?"

74

Stephanie nodded.

"And secondly . . ." she poured a glass for each of them, "I'm just as bad as everybody else. I'm dying to know what happened to you and JD last weekend at the Gorge."

Stephanie laughed. So that's why she was asked to stay.

"Am I terrible?" Kay made a repentant face. "Garth told me that JD is taking this very hard. Maybe I can help some way."

Stephanie believed her. She looked concerned.

"The thing that worries me most," Stephanie began between bites, "is that it's preying on JD's mind. I can get scared, too, all over again, by thinking about it, but I . . ." she groped for a way to say it, then ended lamely, "just don't think about it all the time. He does!"

"Maybe JD's experience was different enough from yours," Kay suggested.

"It was! He had the amnesia. I'm sure that bothers him. And the camera disappearing without a trace. He got a lot closer than I did, trying to get a picture. Maybe he's suffering from radioactivity or something we don't know anything about."

"The people who came over from the other camp," Kay began, rearranging her plate and glass. "Did you get their address so they could confirm seeing that scorched area?"

Stephanie's face fell. "No," she said. Neither she nor JD had thought of that. "They had Colorado license plates," she remembered hopefully, then realized how ridiculous that sounded. It was like saying they had brown eyes.

"I'm not sure they believed us," Stephanie added sadly. "At least JD thinks they didn't."

"But they saw the place it landed," Kay persisted.

"It was a perfect circle, Mrs. Eagleton. And the ground had

been torn up, but smoothly, like someone had taken a giant spoon and scooped up the grass and dirt then pressed it down again every which-way. I even thought it smelled strange, like it was burned, you know."

"Then someone even now could see the circle."

"JD would like to go back. But I wouldn't," Stephanie shivered.

"Does JD still think he was taken inside the UFO?"

"Does he what?"

Kay looked puzzled. "He told Garth he was *in* it."

"*In the UFO?*" The hair stood along Stephanie's arms. "Did he say that?"

"Well . . . yes," she cleared her throat, "I hope I'm not telling something I shouldn't. Hasn't he said anything to you?"

"No," she barely whispered the word, returning now to what she'd heard him saying in his sleep. "You mean the amnesia really wasn't amnesia? He remembers something else?"

"Garth said it came to JD like a flash, that he *saw* something inside the UFO that made him think he'd been inside it."

"Oh, no," Stephanie felt herself trembling, "no wonder he's having nightmares. Why didn't he tell me?"

"I'm sorry. I didn't realize . . ."

"It's okay. I just don't know what to think now."

Then Stephanie was even more upset to see Kay upset. Neither one of them finished her cake. Kay got up, as if she knew Stephanie couldn't talk about it any more right then. She walked into her living room and brought two paperbacks to the kitchen. "I had these in stock," she said, showing her one book entitled *UFO: Affirmative,* the other with a cover picture of a glowing object hovering over a city street. "I think it will help you both, especially JD, to know more about the subject. I've read these myself, and I'm convinced. Go ahead," she held out the books. "Take time to read these. It's normal to fear what we don't understand."

Stephanie looked at Kay gratefully and took the books she offered. The phone in the living room rang just at that moment, and Stephanie was glad for the chance to get into her parka. She was stunned by what Kay had told her. She wanted to be by herself to think about it.

"She's almost ready to leave, Mrs. Anderson. May I give her a message?" She paused. "Yes, just a minute. It's for you, Stephanie. It's your mother."

Kay walked politely out of the room and into the kitchen. Stephanie could see her putting the dishes in the sink. For some reason, she was glad Kay couldn't hear what her mother was saying. There was a man at the house, a Mr. Hank Corrigan, from some UFO organization. He had read about them in the *Times* and wanted to talk to Stephanie now, if she was ready to come home. Stephanie kept her reactions to herself and merely listened. She took in a deep breath when her mother had finished.

"Okay, Mom, I'll be right there. I'm leaving now."

NINE

Hank Corrigan waited in his car in front of the Anderson's house, going through the papers in his briefcase. He'd wanted to get back to Denver Saturday—he'd promised Robbie a hockey game—but now he'd have to wait and make the drive Sunday morning. He hoped the story that led him here would be worth investigating.

Corrigan had picked up a copy of the *Red Butte Times* yesterday in Rock Springs. Like many geologists, he spent his share of Friday nights in motels away from his family and he usually ended up reading the kind of junk to be found around motel offices. He'd supposed the local newspaper he bought for a quarter wouldn't be any different. Then he'd seen the headline, upper right on the front page: *Red Butte Kids See UFO*. The item was written by the teen-age boy himself with an earnestness that convinced Corrigan he might find a real sighting here and not another hoax.

It was Hank's business—and he frankly enjoyed it more than the job that paid him a salary—to investigate UFO reports for the National Investigations Committee on Aerial Phenomena, known generally as NICAP. Normally his investigations were made with a subcommittee, but while he was

79

in the "neighborhood," he thought he might as well check this one out. Besides, the account had excited him. There were two witnesses, there was little chance on Skull Mountain for confusing what they'd seen with aircraft, Venus had been in its evening cycle, and the close-range encounter was still enough of a rarity to be provocative.

Mr. Corrigan looked up from the *Times* account, which he'd been re-reading, to see a slender blond girl in a red parka and blue jeans hurrying along the sidewalk about a block away. He wondered if this could be Stephanie. She swung a purse at her side and studied the ground intently as she walked. She didn't seem at all self-conscious. She'd be easy to talk to—if she was the one. Seconds later as she turned up the drive with only a sideways glance at his car, he knew he'd been right.

He gave the girl and her mother a few seconds alone, then straightened his tie and got out of the car. Mrs. Anderson met him at the door and invited him in. This time, when she offered coffee, he accepted.

Mrs. Anderson, looking flushed and nervous, seated Mr. Corrigan on the living room sofa and encouraged him to spread out his papers right there on the coffee table. She moved a plant and a stack of newspapers out of the way and pulled up a captain's chair that might have been more at home in the kitchen.

"This interview doesn't exclude you, Mrs. Anderson," Hank offered, though he got his best results when a kid's parents were out of the way.

"I haven't started dinner," she smiled. "I have plenty to do in the kitchen."

He wondered what had happened to Stephanie until he

heard water running upstairs. Of course she'd have to fix up, he reminded himself. His own Debbie, thirteen, could spend an hour getting ready just to say "hello" to the boy who delivered groceries. He hoped Stephanie wasn't planning to take a bath first!

Then, as he heard her step on the stairs, Mrs. Anderson came back with his coffee and an ash tray. "Will you be comfortable now?"

"Fine, fine. You're very nice to serve me coffee after barging in on you like this."

"Well, I'm glad to. Make yourself at home. Stephanie," she turned to her daughter, "this is Mr. Corrigan. He's here all the way from Denver to see you and JD." It wasn't quite the truth, but that had been the easiest thing to tell her.

"Is JD coming home from work?" Stephanie asked. Hopefully, Hank thought.

"No," Mr. Corrigan explained, opening his briefcase, "I'll stop over there to have dinner and see him afterward."

"Oh," it sounded flat.

"We'd really rather interview you separately," he offered her a fatherly smile.

"To see if we're . . ." he thought she was going to say "lying," but she stopped before the word came out.

"Separate viewpoints are important. We get more information this way. And, of course, we don't expect descriptions to be identical. You know the old story about the four blind men and the elephant . . ."

"Yes," she seemed to get the point.

It took another minute to set up his tape recorder. He'd expected her to be a bit of a chatterbox, but she was clearly waiting for him to begin. Close enough now to see the freckles on her face, he also noticed that she was feeling uneasy. She held tight to the chair arms and he was afraid she might forget to breathe.

"This won't be as bad as going to the dentist," he grinned.

"Are you sure?" He was glad to hear her laugh.

"Yup! And if you'd rather I didn't tape this, I'll be happy just to take notes."

"No, it won't bother me," she assured him.

He remembered an old farmer in western Nebraska throwing them out of the house when they'd set up the recording device without any explanation. "Get on outta here!" the old man shouted. "Ain't nobody goin' to ridicule me!" They'd learned their lesson.

Then Mr. Corrigan explained what NICAP was and how their records were kept confidential. Without Stephanie's express permission, no part of their interview could be used or made public. He felt like the cop on TV giving the criminal his "rights" speech.

"In fact," he went on, "the first question I'll ask is if you're giving me this information of your own free will, if the answers are unrehearsed and to the best of your knowledge and memory, true."

"At any time you like," he went on, "we can interrupt. If you need a rest, a glass of water, a walk around the block, we'll switch it off until you're ready to go on. Okay?"

Stephanie nodded and he turned on the tape recorder. They went through the preliminaries, then he handed her a questionnaire and asked if she'd like to discuss the UFO incident in the order of the questions suggested there.

At first her voice was tight and high-pitched, but as they started through the list of questions, she seemed to relax. Later on, when her excitement increased, it wasn't the interview jitters, he realized. It was the excitement of actual recall. Stephanie had decidedly feared for her life and her brother's.

She got through the descriptions of sound and color and movement. She had no trouble with the multi-colored lights or their direction, but she couldn't remember other distinguishing details. The UFO had been blindingly bright, she explained.

Describing the size of the UFO in relation to something familiar seemed to be harder. Mr. Corrigan asked her a second time to make a comparison.

"Well, I guess it was as big as our house, but not as high. Like one story, I suppose. Or as big as our backyard if it were round instead of square."

He frowned. Almost everyone who reported seeing a UFO found comparisons difficult. If only people had some orientation *before* they had the experience.

"When it was hovering over the power lines, did it appear to be, say, twice the height of the poles or half the height?" he persisted.

"I really don't know. I was too scared. You see, I thought the moon had exploded at first, then I was afraid the world had come to an end. I just couldn't think." She twisted a strand of her hair into a tight rope against her cheek. He wouldn't press any further on that one. As she herself had said, JD would be able to answer those questions better than she could.

"Azimuth of object" she also left to JD, but since she alone had seen the final maneuvering, he asked her to be very specific in the rest of her answers.

"How long would you say it sat there in the clearing?"

"Hmmm," she puzzled, "JD had said we were camping about a mile inside the gate. And it was dark, so I stumbled around . . . I didn't see it leave until I was almost at the Morrises' camper," she was thinking out loud. Then she looked up. "I'd say it took off twenty minutes after we first saw it, maybe even thirty."

"And it changed color," she had almost forgotten, "when I looked back, the thing had become a glowing whitish color, just as it lifted up from the ground."

"Like fluorescent light?" He finished his coffee and set the cup and saucer back on the table.

"Maybe," she frowned, "but it was actually a color I've never seen before."

Hank could have said those words for her, he'd heard them so often in interviews. Colors, speeds, maneuverings of UFO's were unlike anything people had seen before. It made their attempts to be scientific nearly impossible.

"Then how did it 'take off'?" Hank went on, quoting her.

"Straight up," Stephanie sat forward. "You wouldn't believe it. It kind of hung there—it must have been up from the ground a way because I could see it over the trees—then it just flew straight up. In maybe three, four seconds it was a pinpoint. Then it disappeared."

"And according to the report in the *Times*, you thought it had taken your brother."

She half smiled. "Yeah, I did. That sounds dumb now."

"No, not at all." This is a really appealing girl, Hank thought. "Well," he moved toward the tape recorder, intending to give her a breather, "have we covered everything?"

"Did I mention the spinning?"

"No."

"As I started down the road, I thought the UFO looked like it was spinning, but it was so bright I couldn't tell if the whole thing was or if part of it was. And maybe I didn't see what I thought I did."

"You mean spinning . . . like a top?"

"Yes, but it's very vague. Maybe I shouldn't mention something I'm not positively sure of."

"It's okay. It might give us a clue."

When Hank Corrigan finally packed up his material and left, he realized he'd been right to follow his hunch. He hoped meeting JD wouldn't change his impression. He'd go back to the Holiday Inn now, listen to the tape, take a few notes, then shower and shave for dinner.

Driving through town to the main street, past older houses haphazardly set on lots to accommodate gardens and chicken sheds, Hank Corrigan fought back an unpleasant tug of nostalgia. In spite of having some hazy, romantic notions to the contrary, he didn't think he could stand to live in one of these small Wyoming towns again. For one thing, the wind blew all the time. The gutters today were a veritable parade of dancing papers and cigarette butts. It looked to him like an empty beer can could make several trips up and down Center Street before a passing car flattened it. Maybe he'd become a snob, but the lack of esthetics in Red Butte depressed him. Of course, he'd lived in Denver awhile now and he liked it, even the big city pace.

"There's no rush or bustle here, for sure," he thought, driving toward the freeway cut-off without seeing another car.

Small town relationships being what they were, he could imagine how the tongues had wagged when the UFO piece appeared in the *Times*. Seeing UFO's was too highly irregular for a place like Red Butte. But the kids were young. They'd survive the talk and the skepticism.

As he pulled into the Holiday Inn, he reminded himself to call Tom Crawford and the police chief to get their reactions. He thought it would be a good idea to talk to JD's boss and the woman Stephanie worked for, too, while he was here. He might not get back through Red Butte until spring.

TEN

JD hated like the devil to ask one more favor of Bob Gillispie. He knew the man from NICAP would be coming in for the interview during the evening, but he hadn't been able to catch Gillispie alone to tell him. Sylvie said she and Jerry would cover for him, but his boss was going to be snorting mad anyway.

For three days now the Holiday Inn dining room had more than its normal traffic of school-aged kids. And they all wanted to talk to JD—or look at him. Several older couples had detained him in conversation when he should have been working, and at least a half-dozen times the phone had rung for him. There was nothing he could do about it but say he was sorry.

"It'll blow over." Sylvie had taken his side when Gillispie chewed him out in the kitchen. "Mind your own business!" she'd been told. "I hire my help to work, not to stand around lollygaggin'. If you're gonna have the flying saucer fever, do it on your own time."

"Yes, sir," JD had managed, but his jaws were working. As if he could help it because the whole town flipped out! And now this, an interview on working hours with a guy whose

name he'd forgotten. Hell, Gillispie would have a hemor-
rhage!

During a brief lull around seven, JD caught his boss looking absently out the vestibule windows toward the parking
lot. "Mr. Gillispie?" he approached him. The older man
turned around. He just frowns automatically, JD thought.
Push-a-button, get-a-scowl! "Could I talk to you a minute?"

Gillispie glanced beyond him to the dining room. "Your
tables all cleared? Coffee brought out?"

"Yes, I'm caught up."

"Well, what is it?"

"My mom called a while ago and said this man—he's a re-
porter or an investigator or something, staying here at the Inn
—wanted to talk to me tonight. He's supposed to come in for
dinner, I guess . . ." his voice trailed off.

"JD, what did I tell you when you came to work today? On
your own time, not mine!"

"Yeah, I know. But I didn't arrange this. He's coming," JD
gestured helplessly, "I don't even *want* to talk to him. So
what do I do?"

Mr. Gillispie shushed JD and steered him toward the
kitchen.

"If he's coming here to eat, you'll have to see him. If I say
you can't, it makes me look like a bastard and the restaurant
gets a black eye. I tell you, JD, any more of this and it'll be
cheaper for me to replace you."

"Well, it hasn't been all that bad for business," JD reminded him with a grin. Immediately he wished he hadn't
said it. Mr. Gillispie's look was as cold as iced crab. "Take
half pay tonight. Ask Jerry to cover and you can quit whenever you damn well please. Remember, this is the last time. I
won't put up with it."

JD hurried back through the kitchen and fed the dirty plates into the dishwasher, his blood pressure steadying a bit now that it was over. What a lot of crap I take, he thought, to have a car to drive. And after that was paid for, college. He wondered if it was worth it.

There were two men already seated singly when he returned to the dining room. The one nearest the door looked like he belonged in Wyoming. The other was wearing a brown business suit and expensive shoes, but Sylvie was taking his order so JD couldn't see the man's face right away. In a few minutes he'd be too busy to worry. Once a month the ranchers met in town with the Co-op for a standing order of steaks and fries; it was always a big job afterward to hustle the mess out to the kitchen and re-arrange the tables.

JD felt the closer man's eyes on him as he worked. He knew he was being sized up. Then, Sylvie stopped him just inside the swinging kitchen doors and confirmed it.

"It's the bimbo in the brown suit."

"You sure?"

"He asked which one was the Anderson boy."

"What am I supposed to do?" JD asked. Sylvie gave him a little shove back toward the dining room. "Work, remember? No lollygaggin'!"

The ranchers at the long table had risen to leave. JD set up his tray and started stacking the dishes. Now the man who had asked for him seemed too busy with his salad to notice what JD was doing. Later on, having coffee, he produced a copy of the *Denver Post* and sat reading for fifteen minutes. JD began to think he might not have an interview after all. When the man left the dining room, paper under his arm, JD felt positively relieved. He was going to get a break. Then he saw Bob Gillispie, an unaccustomed smile pasted on his face, coming toward him across the room. The man in the brown suit was close behind.

"Hank Corrigan," Gillispie introduced them, "this is JD Anderson. He'd like to talk to you here, JD, so why don't you change into your street clothes and I'll have Sylvie bring you both some hot coffee."

JD couldn't believe his ears. The old sonofabitch was really laying it on. Well, that's business, he told himself, cynically. He had a fleeting vision of snapping his fingers at Sylvie for service, but decided he'd better not do that.

JD was surprised at how easy Mr. Corrigan was to talk to. They followed a list of questions for the most part and the researcher, as he called himself, took a few notes. He'd written down the Morrises' names, then seemed disappointed that JD didn't know where they could be reached. The only other time Mr. Corrigan seemed disturbed by an answer was when JD said he estimated the UFO remained in the clearing an hour or more. At the end of the questions he asked JD to repeat that again, although he'd taken it down in his notes earlier.

Since last weekend JD had read in the *Saucer Review* about other cars stalling out in the vicinity of UFO's and so he was eager to ask Corrigan, as much of an expert as he'd ever meet, what his theory about it was. The answer was disappointing. "We just don't know," he said flatly. "Engines die. Lights go out. It happens repeatedly. But not always. This inconsistency is what makes it so hard for us to establish patterns. Every report, like yours, is an individual case; it may jibe with other sightings or it may not."

"I guess UFO's appear in all different shapes and sizes," JD went on, wishing he could ask the hundred questions that popped into his mind.

"I've talked to people who've seen the cigar shape, which

someone else might refer to as cylindrical. The saucer shape, oval, football shapes are fairly common. But it's interesting that they fall within those fairly narrow limits. It's a rarity to have a flying boxcar or a pyramid reported, for instance."

"Yeah, I see what you mean."

"JD," Mr. Corrigan looked uneasily toward the hostess who had been kept hopping all evening. "I think we're taking up space here. Would you mind coming back to my room to put a couple of answers on tape? Have you got fifteen more minutes?"

"Sure," JD slid out of the booth, leaving a nickel tip under the saucer for Sylvie to cry over. "Mr. Gillispie let me off early tonight." He felt like adding "with half pay," but thought better of it.

Seated on a small sofa in Mr. Corrigan's room, JD watched him open a bottle and mix himself a nightcap. "An old Wyoming custom," he winked. He offered JD a soft drink, but it didn't sound good right then. With the tape recorder set up, JD gave his name and address and attested to his own truthfulness. They went back over four or five of the important questions and then Mr. Corrigan switched off the tape and stretched out in the easy chair.

"Someday maybe it'll happen to me," he smiled. "I'd like a trip to Venus out of it, like George Adamski claimed he got."

"You mean you've never seen a UFO?" JD couldn't believe it. "Then why are you doing this for NICAP?"

"It's interesting. Or maybe I'm curious. You don't conduct many interviews before you join ranks with the believers. I've heard some stories of actual landings, JD, that would make your hair stand on end. And then there are the contact stories . . ."

"What do you mean?"

"Well, a meeting in which there was intentional contact, supposedly. Some people believe they've been given messages. From the humanoids, as we call them."

"Has anybody ever claimed to be taken into a UFO?" JD asked, feeling his way.

"Oh, yes. There's a recent case in Mississippi. And the men's story held up under hypnosis and repeated questioning. There's another one from New England that has a lot of validity in my mind. Perfectly reliable people with high I.Q.s, a man and his wife, think they were taken aboard a UFO and examined."

"Let me ask you," JD noticed his hands were sweating. "During the time I blacked out, you know . . . is it possible that those humanoids could have taken me in that UFO?"

Mr. Corrigan sat forward and put his drink on the table. "Do you have reason to believe that?"

"No," JD answered quickly, opting for a half lie. "No, I just wondered, you know, if something like that could happen to a person without his knowing it."

Mr. Corrigan didn't look convinced.

"Do you *suspect*," he emphasized the word, "something further happened to you during that time?"

JD squirmed. "You see, I don't know. I felt pretty terrible all that next day. My skin felt funny. My hands and face, where I wasn't covered, got kind of tingly."

"I've heard similar reports from another sub-committee I'm in touch with. Close encounters have produced quite a variety of symptoms."

"Like dizziness?"

Corrigan nodded.

"And nausea?"

He nodded again. Then there was a long, finally uncomfortable silence in the room. JD wondered if they were finished, but when Mr. Corrigan stood up, he was only after more ice.

"And you still can't remember anything that happened during the time the UFO was there in the clearing, after you approached it? How long a time period was that again?"

"An hour, I guess," JD was saying it for the third time. "But it's hard to say when you have a mind blank that way. I felt like it had been about an hour before I recognized Stephanie standing over me."

"You know," Corrigan sat down once more, shaking the ice around in his glass. "There are a lot of different theories. Some UFOlogists believe there's mental control from the operators of the UFO's over the human beings they encounter."

"You mean to make a person forget everything?"

"Yes, or to perform a certain way. Possibly even to be so confused he'll never make sense to anyone."

JD wished he could tell him. He had liked Mr. Corrigan from the start. He also liked being treated like an adult. He thought of Mr. Grosbeck and Bob Gillispie and Lenny Jones. They were so used to thinking of him as a kid, they never shifted gears to anything else. He guessed that was what he liked about Garth. He wasn't forever putting him down. Maybe he should level with Mr. Corrigan, he was thinking, and tell him what had kept him from sleeping for a week. He'd never have a better chance.

Mr. Corrigan didn't look surprised when JD opened up and told him about the "vision" he'd seen at Garth's house and the terrifying dreams he'd had since.

"I haven't told anyone else, not even Stephanie," he admitted. "It's just too crazy to tell anybody, but it really bothers me. Sometimes at school, I can't think about anything else. I don't even hear what the teacher's saying."

"What happens in the dreams?" Mr. Corrigan asked.

"I keep dreaming the same thing. I'm running toward the UFO and I can't stop. I'm drawn to it like a magnet, then suddenly these 'men' have me by the arms and are forcing me into a room somewhere. Then I wake up in a sweat, and I'm scared to go back to sleep again."

"Does the nightmare begin with you running?"

"No. It always starts when I've focused in on the UFO with my camera. I have it in my view finder. Then I start running and I'm, like, mesmerized. I can't stop." JD found himself rubbing the back of one hand with the other. Suddenly he realized his hands were tingling again and the sensation was creeping up his neck.

"God!" he gasped, "nothing like this ever happened to me before!"

"Boy, I'm sorry," Corrigan said, "it's damned unnerving! I had no idea when I interviewed Stephanie that your encounter would be so much more . . . subjective."

JD wasn't sure he knew what Mr. Corrigan was saying, but his voice was sympathetic.

"Maybe you should see a doctor if the nightmares continue. A sedative might help temporarily. But I can hardly suggest you tell him why you need it . . ." He sounded cynical. JD could see why.

"The best thing for you to do now, in my opinion, is to try to forget the whole experience. You can't let it eat on you, JD. And you can't make sense out of it for yourself either. In a place like Red Butte, where everybody likes to know everybody's business and where even the imaginations are provincial, this story of yours won't buy you anything but ridicule."

Then Mr. Corrigan recalled for JD other cases from his experience—the patrolman chased by a UFO who lost his job and his wife, then ended up in a mental institution. "Catatonic schizophrenic" was the diagnosis. He remembered the minister he'd interviewed who now worked at a Safeway vegetable counter in Cincinnati and still talks about seeing "creatures." The most poignant case for him was one he'd read about. A young boy in North Dakota had become a virtual recluse after his UFO photographs were called "frauds" and "double exposures" by the press.

It was getting late. When Mr. Corrigan finally stood up and rinsed out his glass at the sink, JD realized it was time to go. He put on his coat, the two of them exchanged thanks and good-bys, and Mr. Corrigan gave him his business card. When they shook hands at the door of the motel room, JD saw himself in the older man's eyes. They were kin, now, in a strange way. He wasn't entirely alone.

"Let's keep in touch," Mr. Corrigan said, gripping JD's hand. "Good luck to both you kids."

ELEVEN

"If we didn't have Sunday morning breakfasts, I'd never see this family all together," Addie Anderson said as she served up a platter of vanilla-smelling French toast from the stove. She had protected her best dress with the oversized apron Stephanie made in home ec. but refused to wear.

"I love Sunday morning, too," Stephanie snuggled into herself. "I adore sleeping in."

"You should go to Sunday school once in a while," her mom scolded.

"She's a church school drop-out," JD said. "She'll probably go straight to hell if she doesn't shape up. Pass the butter, please."

"JD!" His mother thumped him on the head.

"What about you?" Stephanie accused. "You only go to church when Gayle makes you. That's worse."

"You're right. I'm a hypocrite," he admitted and hoisted a monstrous chunk of French toast to his mouth.

"If you kids had grown up the way I did," their father said, "you'd have gone every Sunday whether you liked it or not. I stoked the furnace at the Methodist Church there in Big Piney and, I tell you, I had to stick around to warm up afterward. I heard all the sermons once and some of them over again."

"You sure had it rough, Dad," JD joshed as he handed the syrup across the table to his father.

"Oh, get on with feeding your face. Your time's coming!"

JD liked Sunday mornings at home, too, but he didn't feel like rhapsodizing about it right then. What was really on his mind was telling his folks the Evanses had invited him to dinner. It was the first time. He and Gayle had been going together for over a year, but he'd never been asked to a meal at their house. He could bring Gayle home, even unannounced. That seemed to be okay. His mom would send him out for more hamburger or she'd cut the roast thinner or somehow make five salad helpings out of four. The Evans' lives were too well organized, he guessed, for drop-in dinner company. He'd wondered if it was Gayle's idea, this invitation, or if—since his celebrity status—they were uncontrollably curious like everyone else. The unlucky appearance of the UFO was now three weeks behind them and in the last few days things seemed to be returning to normal. Thank God, JD sighed. The headaches had gone away. And the nightmares were less frequent. They were just as real when they came, however, stalking through the night walls of his room.

"You finally caught up with your hours at work?" his father broke into his thoughts.

"Finally," he answered. "I'm off all day today. Gayle and I may drive out to Dougan's to see if they'll let us ride horses for a while."

"Have you done anything about that scholarship application?" Addie asked.

"Not yet."

"You need the scholarship, JD."

"You can say that again." The amount he owed on the car, $970.88, flashed to mind. Where responsibility was concerned, he wished he could trade places with Stephanie. Fifteen was pure paradise. The only money he'd needed then was for a movie or a weekend game of pool with Chic. Maybe, he thought, depressed by it all, "his time *had* come" as his dad was forever predicting.

"Gayle's rich daddy can pay every penny of her tuition," Stephanie needled.

"Working in a bank doesn't automatically make you rich," JD sneered. "All that money in the First National isn't his to spend, you know."

"I'm not that dumb! But everyone knows the Evanses are" —she struck a fancy pose—"well off!" It came out sounding like a social disease.

"So?" JD got up to refill his juice glass. Stephanie could be snotty when it came to Gayle. "Anyway," he went on, "they asked me to dinner."

"They *what*?" his mother looked shocked. "To dinner? At their house?"

"Uh huh."

"Ooh, neat!" Stephanie gloated. "Remember what you have to eat. I want a Julia Child description of every crumb."

"Are you going to accept?" John, Sr., asked. He looked JD straight in the eye.

"Of course he will!" Stephanie butted in. "Why wouldn't he?"

JD returned his father's look. Innately suspicious of bankers anyway, the old man had a particular dislike for Charlie Evans. He'd lost $40,000 on the sale of his ranch because of an invalid contract handled by Mr. Evans, president and financial counselor at Red Butte's only lending institution. Then when JD borrowed money for the used car from First National, his dad had practically gone out of his mind. He'd refused to co-sign. He wouldn't even talk about it. But Charlie Evans, on the strength of JD's job and good school record, made an exception and loaned him the $1,600. He'd offered to be the co-signer himself. JD thought at the time that Gayle had probably wheedled her father into it. Now, by unspoken agreement, they never brought up Charlie Evans' name at home.

"I don't know if I'll go or not." JD lowered his eyes.

"JD, you have to," Stephanie acted like she could hardly stand it. "I'd go if they invited me."

"Well, they didn't." Sometimes he wished she'd just shut up.

"When do they want you to come?" his mother asked.

"Next Friday. That's the problem. I'm supposed to work."

"You know why they asked you?" his father was still pushing the point.

"I can guess."

"I wouldn't go," John stated, flat out. "I wouldn't give them a minute, if it was me. A whole year and you haven't been good enough to sit at their table. Now that you're a topic of conversation around town, you're suddenly okay. You think about it, JD."

He was. He was thinking about it.

Addie stirred her coffee extra hard. She got nervous at the first hint of a family fight. "He'll have to make up his own mind, John. It's not for us to decide."

"Wait and see," her husband coughed, shoving himself back from the table. "Wait and see what happens," he could hardly say it for the wheezing spell that came on. "I tell you" —he struggled to get his breath—"they want some kicks, that's all." Finally, when he reached the other room, they heard the coughing subside. JD wished he hadn't said anything at all.

JD studied the syrup left on his plate, then shoved back his chair, too. It wasn't that he'd have to swallow his own pride to go. He owed Mr. Evans more than money for that loan. No one else would have given it to him. And Gayle. She'd acted so pleased when she handed him the little note her mother had written. He didn't want to hurt her feelings.

"Maybe Bob Gillispie won't let me off the hook," JD said, to no one in particular. "It might all be decided for me—"

The air was snappy with cold when JD left home the next Friday night to walk to Gayle's. He'd been keyed up all day. Walking would do him good. Besides, Gayle had promised to meet him so they could be alone a few minutes before the dinner party, as Mrs. Evans called it.

His dad hadn't said anything about the invitation since Sunday. JD knew he was trying not to interfere, even though the association with Charlie Evans galled him so much he could hardly stand it. Actually, having to ask off work had tortured JD more than anything else. Bob Gillispie had laid down the law twice already.

As it turned out, Mr. Evans had called Gillispie and personally asked if JD could get off Friday night. "'We've planned our whole evening around JD Anderson!'" Gillispie had mimicked Charlie Evans talking to him on the phone. "'We're having other guests who count on seeing him.' Hell," he'd gone on, slamming a lid on the iron pot. "Look what you got yourself into with that crazy UFO story!"

JD had simply stood there, waiting for what his boss would say next. The answer could be yes, no, or kiss off! Charlie

Evans was a big man in Red Butte, but Gillispie with his pinched mind and nasty disposition wouldn't like being shoved around by influence.

"Could I work Sunday instead of Friday? Would it make that much difference?" JD asked.

"The difference is that I can't count on you anymore. I don't want help who has to play games with the schedule all the time. I'm trying to run a business here."

In the end, Gillispie had told him to go, but also warned that he was on probation. Any more shenanigans and he could look for work somewhere else.

Now, thinking over their conversation, JD wondered who the other guests were. That part he hadn't told his folks. "Some damn circus," his dad would've said. "And you the main attraction . . ." No, he could do without that. Mr. Evans must have really wanted him for dinner, to go to so much trouble.

Gayle met JD about three blocks from her house and they slowed to a snail's pace, holding hands and walking close. JD noticed how choice she looked tonight, how the white turtleneck brushed the roundness of her chin and set off her adorable, incomparable, irresistible face. As usual, he walked a foot taller with her beside him.

They stopped to kiss under a street lamp for the whole world to see. Then they laughed at the way their frosty breath hung in the air, making them look like characters talking on a comic strip.

Finally they rounded the corner where Gayle lived.

"Are you nervous?" she teased, turning merry eyes on him.

"I guess. A little," he grinned. "What if I drop my fork or something stupid?"

"Then I'll drop mine."

"With my luck I'll probably drop my spoon, too."

"So will I then!"

"Let's follow that by chucking our knives under the table, okay? And we'll make loud noises with the celery."

"You struck out. We're not having celery," she stood on her tiptoes and pecked him on the cheek. "Dummy!"

"Who's going to be there besides me?" He thought he might as well know now.

"Dr. and Mrs. Burke," she paused, "you know Dr. Burke—"

"Yeah. He's new at the hospital. Dad's seen him a few times."

"And Tom Gordon. His wife was coming, too, but one of their kids was sick."

"Who's he?"

"You don't know Tom Gordon?"

"Why should I?"

"He's that communicastor from Casper. My mom listens to him all the time on his talk show."

"I guess I've heard him once or twice."

"Every day, nine to twelve, my mom listens to him. It's nauseating."

"Is he a friend of the family?" JD was still trying to figure out where he himself fit into this dinner arrangement.

"He and daddy were at Laramie together, at the U. Fraternity brothers and all that. Daddy says he's getting too liberal for us, but we still have dinner with them when we go to Laramie for the football games." She squeezed his hand tight in both of hers. "Come on, now, just relax, JD, and be your charming old self."

"I'm charming, all right," he laughed. And then they were there, standing exactly where JD had stood hundreds of times before to ring the bell. Impulsively, he pulled Gayle back into the shadows of two large arbor vitae. Laughing softly, she got her hands inside his coat and slipped her arms around him, nestling against his chest. Her kisses were as warm and greedy as ever. He hoped his last-minute hoarding would carry him through the evening.

"Oh, here you are!" Mr. Evans met them at the wide double doors of the den. He shook hands with JD and clapped him on the shoulder. "Glad to see you!"

JD mumbled his thanks and allowed the older man to take his coat. Inside the room, the fire was blazing, drinks had been passed around, and it sounded like the evening was well underway. Mrs. Evans gave him a polite hug, then told Gayle to fix them some ginger ale. In the meantime, she introduced JD around and invited him to sit close to the fire in a comfortable leather arm chair that looked suspiciously like the seat of honor. He'd have preferred being by Gayle on the sofa, but he guessed now he was strictly on his own.

Everyone made small talk and exchanged pleasantries while Gayle passed a tray of little meat and cheese things. So far the fraternity man Tom Gordon was leading the only conversation going, and Gayle's mom was hanging on his every word. Mrs. Burke, plump and smily, seemed to size up JD's discomfort and began asking questions about school. They were the usual. What grade was he in? Would he be glad to graduate? What was he planning to go into? She was nice and much more attractive than her husband who looked like a prune. JD wondered if doctors aged faster than other people.

Before long, the inevitable happened. Tom Gordon turned the conversation to JD and the UFO sighting.

"I read a note about your adventure in the *Casper Star*, JD. Yours is getting to be a household name around these parts."

"I hope not!" JD protested.

"You don't like being in the limelight?" Tom laughed, like he'd been in the center of things forever and knew all about it.

"Not me," JD shook his head, already feeling sticky.

"You know, that piece in the *Times* was very well written. If you're going into journalism, like Gayle says, you've got all the natural equipment for it."

"Thanks," JD managed.

"He wrote a very impressive editorial on human rights for the school paper." Gayle smiled prettily at Tom. "It was a Pulitzer Prize winner!"

"Yeah? How about that?" Tom turned to Charlie Evans and gestured with his pipe. "They oughta give a Student Pulitzer, hadn't they? I think I'll suggest that next time the committee's in session." Mrs. Evans laughed.

"JD," it was the doctor's turn. "I was talking with Mrs. Eagleton, and she said you'd been having some terrific headaches since that night at the Gorge."

"They're gone now. For good, I hope."

"Do you think they were associated with seeing what you did?"

"They must have been. I never have headaches normally."

"I'd like to hear about that scorched circle on the ground," Charlie Evans said as he put another log on the fire. "Do you mind describing it for Tom here? He was saying that would be a mighty convincing calling card. Fact is, we'd all like to see *that*."

JD felt the adrenalin flow. Somewhere in the back of his

mind the "proceed with caution" placard moved into place. He wasn't sure what direction the conversation would take.

"Well, Stephanie and I paced it off. The diameter was about thirty feet. The ground had been disturbed in a perfect circle. Dirt was turned up, plants pulled up by the roots."

"Could the mark have been made by anything else?" Charlie asked. "Did you consider that?"

"We didn't think of anything else, of course, because we'd seen the UFO right there. We knew that's what made the depression and burned the ground." It seemed perfectly logical to Stephanie and him.

There was silence in the room. JD looked from one face to another. "I know," he made a vague motion with his hands, "it's incredible."

"Was there any evidence of a landing apparatus?" the doctor asked. He might look like a prune, but he asked good questions, JD thought.

"If I'd known then what I know now about UFO's, after reading some books," JD explained, "I might have looked for landing impressions. As it was, no, we didn't notice any."

"What do you think, JD? Are these things space ships from another planet?" Tom inquired.

"I couldn't say," JD shrugged. "Some people do think we're being observed by other beings. I guess it could be happening."

"How can they believe that and still hold to our Christian traditions?" Mrs. Evans asked. "I think we've got enough problems right here"—she turned to Mrs. Burke to make her point—"without worrying about space visitors spying on us."

"We can't ignore the possibilities, though," Tom continued. "Carl, do you remember the study made at Green Bank,

West Virginia? Back, oh, somewhere in the early sixties? I was still in Washington—"

"Green Bank?" Dr. Burke frowned. "Vaguely—"

"Well, anyhow, these scientists got together—it was top secret stuff, you know—and they decided there were likely many civilizations of highly intelligent inhabitants out there. They came up with an outside figure somewhere around fifty million!"

Mr. Evans shook his head, even while Tom was talking. "Maybe I have too much ego, but I can't go along with that. Human beings are supposed to be the crowning of creation, aren't they?"

"We don't always act so regal," Mrs. Burke said quietly. JD smiled his agreement.

"Coming back to that patch on the ground there at Skull Mountain," Dr. Burke turned to JD. "It's not going to change much over winter if it's the way you described it. You ought to go up next spring and see what you can find."

"I plan to. And next time I'll chain myself to my camera."

"Take another witness," Tom suggested, "besides your sister, that is. For corroboration."

"I think Garth Magleby will go up with me."

"JD," Mr. Evans said, pausing for everyone's attention, "we were talking before you got here. We wondered if you and Stephanie might have seen a meteorite."

JD couldn't believe his ears.

"Approach it this way," Mr. Evans spread his hands in explanation. "What natural phenomenon did that thing most closely resemble? And then take it from there. Could what you saw have been something explainable? Something in the realm of nature?"

Gayle joined the conversation from her place on the sofa. "It was something you didn't recognize, so you called it a UFO. Couldn't it have been something *else* you'd never seen before?"

"Like what?" JD asked. "What big glowing object sits on a power pole, floats across space, then lands without making a sound? Meteorites don't float. They streak! And whoever saw a meteorite shoot back into the sky again? Ball lightning, if you're thinking of that, is about the size of a grapefruit, isn't it?"

"In rare cases," Dr. Burke said, "a meteor can actually appear to move upward, up from the horizon of the witness. I'm not saying this was the case here."

Mr. Evans laughed. "Sorry, JD, but most of us would have to see it believe it." His daughter shook her head in agreement.

"Oh, I know that," JD admitted. "I'm not going around expecting people to believe me," he looked ruefully at Gayle. She might have trusted him, at least. Whenever he'd brought the subject up, she hadn't wanted to listen. Like seeing the UFO was some kind of heresy. A month ago he'd been perfectly conventional and acceptable. Suddenly, whamo! He was a UFO witness on the lunatic fringe.

"We're not saying we don't believe you," Tom Gordon was sounding like a mediator, "we're just unable to experience in our rational minds what you saw and felt out there."

"I wouldn't believe it, either, if it hadn't happened to me," JD said, feeling the sickness that comes with compromise. Why was he trying to please *them*?

"Doctor," Tom Gordon took the floor, "I realize every sighting is a special case and has to be considered on its own merits—and this isn't directed at you, JD—but are there certain kinds of people more *apt* to see UFO's than others?"

"Well," the doctor crossed his legs and cleared his throat, "I suppose certain antisocial personalities might make up UFO stories for their own gratification."

"What kind of psychopath would be apt to have hallucinations like that?" Mr. Evans asked.

"The ambulatory schizophrenic. Generally speaking, again, of course."

"Let's see now," JD couldn't help saying, "where do Steph and I fit in here?"

Mrs. Burke laughed and leaned over to pat JD's hand. "My husband's using his clinical voice. He's not talking about you!"

JD wasn't sure.

But Dr. Burke wasn't ready to be interrupted. "Another interesting psychosis—suggested by JD's experience—is called *folie à deux*. One person communicates his particular delusions to someone very close to him, husband to wife or one sibling to another, then dominates that person to the extent that they share the same hallucination. The human mind is very complex," he concluded, chuckling and shaking his head.

Mrs. Evans stood and asked Gayle to pass the hors d'oeuvres around the circle of guests. "We'll be eating in a minute," she said, then excused herself. JD would be glad to move into the dining room.

It was Charlie Evans who made the final observation before they left the den. "The Air Force made a twenty-year study and came up with no evidence," he said with authority. "That's good enough for me. 'It's no threat,' they said. If they're not worried, I'm not worried."

The amiable disagreement came from Dr. Burke. "I wouldn't rely on the Air Force or Washington to find the truth about UFO's, Charlie."

"You think so?" Mr. Evans smiled as they stood, clapping the doctor good naturedly on the shoulder.

JD could see the conversation was going to go on through dinner. He didn't know if he could eat. Then they seated Gayle next to him. Normally he would have laughed when she bent close and whispered, "Remember to drop your fork," but he didn't find her remark very funny now. He ignored what she said, pretending to be busy with his napkin.

Somehow JD got through the clear soup and the salad, listening to Tom Gordon tell a story about a guest on his talk show who claimed she and her ailing mother had seen a UFO. "You couldn't shake her," he laughed. "All these people called in—one was an astronomer at the college—but she stuck to her story. She'd taken her mother from the nursing home for a ride and they'd watched this thing for ten minutes, in broad daylight, on the back side of Casper Mountain."

"Did you ever have her mother on the air?" Dr. Burke asked.

"No, I was afraid she might croak right there in the studio, she was so old."

Gayle giggled.

"And no one else saw anything?" Mrs. Burke asked.

"Not that we knew of then. About a month later, a scruffy looking sheepherder stopped by the radio station. He'd been scared to death by a flying saucer swooping over his animals, but he'd forgotten what day it happened. And even though his wagon was on that same south slope, we were never able to confirm anything."

By the time Mrs. Evans brought in the roast beef and Yorkshire pudding, the men had got off onto local politics, a subject close to the hearts and purse-strings of all councilmen like Charlie Evans. When the two women started talking together, JD breathed easier. That left Gayle and him to have their own conversation, but for once they didn't seem to have anything to say. JD ate his roast beef in silence. He may have finished dinner without saying a word, but suddenly there was a noisy clattering on the terrazzo floor. He laughed out loud in spite of himself. He had just knocked his fork off the edge of the table!

A sideways glance, after a decent interval, told him Gayle wasn't about to lose possession of her silverware just to make him feel better.

"Clumsy!" said the look on her face, as she turned back to buttering a roll.

TWELVE

A light December snow had been falling all day, but the highways were still clear when JD and Chic Wilcox left for the basketball game. Chic figured they'd make it if they could follow the school bus all the way into Glenrock. His rebuilt Pontiac was a toss-up even in good weather.

"What'd Gayle say when you told her you were going to the game with me tonight?" Chic asked, shifting down to keep behind the lumbering bus that had just crossed a set of tracks.

"She didn't act like she cared. I'm pissed off at her anyway, and she knows it."

"I can't believe it. Gayle's perfect. You told me so yourself."

"Then I was wrong."

"Lovers' quarrel." Chic diagnosed it in two words. "You'll go running back to one another's arms"—he slid off into his soap opera voice—"passions brimming, full of remorse . . . smack, smack, smack!" he kissed the air.

"Knock it off," JD groaned, "what do you know about it?"

"I took a girl out once."

"Oh, yeah? What happened?"

"She got sick."

"Did you ever tell the truth in your life, Chic?"

"No kidding. I took her to a carnival, and she got sick on the tilt-a-whirl. She puked all over me."

"So you haven't asked a girl out since?"

"Just Bonnie."

"Bonnie who?" JD looked at Chic like he knew this was going to be another fabrication, but to go ahead while he was still enjoying the dialogue.

"Bonnie's my cousin and I have this thing about her. Boy, is she built!" He held his hand out at an appropriate distance from his own flat chest. JD cracked up.

"I think as your best and oldest friend," his best and oldest friend began, "I'd better rescue you. Would you double with Gayle and me some night? Gayle could dig up *someone*," he made it sound nigh impossible.

"Nah. I'm not mature enough for girls. My mother said she'd tell me when I was. Honest, I heard my folks talking the other night. Dad said, 'Damn! You'd think the juices would be flowing by now!' That's what he said." Chic looked at JD like it was all an incomprehensible puzzlement.

"Say, how about Stephanie?" JD said. "She hates sophomore boys. I bet she'd go out with an older man like you. You should hear her! She calls this one guy 'Zits' who's been hanging around. 'Gross' she calls this other kid who asked her to the Christmas Dance. She just told him 'no.' Can you believe it? An out-and-out *no*. Not 'I'm busy' or 'I'm making fudge that night' but just 'no.'"

JD cocked his head, presumably studying Chic's profile. "She'd be just right for you. Stephanie likes someone with intellect."

Chic didn't say anything right away. He'd always liked

Stephanie himself. She used to go on bike hikes with JD and him, and he remembered she was a good sport for a girl. "Stephanie'll be so popular in a year you'll be beating the boys off your porch."

"No," JD persisted. "Come to think of it, I don't know why I didn't think of it sooner. My best friend and my sister! She looks up to you, Chic. She told me once she thought you were a genius."

"Hmmm," Chic considered the stretch of highway ahead of him, trying to bring the "now" Stephanie into focus. She was stuck in his mind's eye at about eleven, with all of eleven's scrawny aspects—elbows, knees, big teeth, and an overwhelming freckle population. When she finally arrived in his mental picture tube, he found himself smiling. "She also has good judgment," he nodded at JD.

It was six-thirty when they arrived in Glenrock, chalking up one more success for the Pontiac. They'd have time for a hamburger and malt before the varsity played. It promised to be a close game. And afterward, there were always the fights to look forward to. Chic had volunteered to be JD's second if they could stir up anything, but he knew JD didn't have the stomach for scrapping with the big, red-faced ranch boys who could throw a bull calf with one hand.

That night the traditional rivals were forced to go into overtime. That was positive assurance of a few bloody battles in the parking lot, even more so after Red Butte made the winning basket. A human interest angle never hurt a sport story, Chic told himself. And his fans at school, who said his column was the only thing they ever read in *The Renegade*, would be expecting some color on this game.

They hung around outside for a while afterward, but it

was awful cold. Other than the exchange of a few choice obscenities, nothing happened. Chic was almost morbid with disappointment. He felt like tripping somebody!

"C'mon, man," JD was dancing on one foot and then another. "We gotta get lined up behind that bus. It's cold as a witch's tit out here."

"Okay, okay," Chic moved reluctantly toward his car, leaving his dream of interschool slaughter lying like a corpse at the door of the gym.

Until they got well out of town, neither of the boys had much to say. When the car heater finally caught up with their body temperature, Chic asked JD what he was thinking about.

"You got Gayle on your mind? You're not sorry you came without her, are you?"

"I wasn't thinking about Gayle."

"That's a giant step." Chic couldn't resist it. As far as he was concerned, Gayle Evans could take a hang glider right off the top of Devil's Tower. He could tolerate losing his best friend to a girl, but losing JD to Gayle in particular was a total rip-off. Gayle made Chic feel ugly. And low class. And inept and graceless and stupid. She could tie his tongue and his wit with one scornful curl of her lip. Mostly, he avoided her, and that meant not seeing JD as well.

"Actually, Chic," JD broke in, "I can't get that UFO out of my head. During the game, with everything that was going on, I was still thinking about that night on the mountain. What's the matter with me?"

"You obsessed or somethin'?"

"God, I don't know. Maybe I'm going bananas."

"What's bugging you? What do you keep thinking about?" Chic had read all the books he could find on the sub-

ject and even sent to the Flying Saucer Society for their litera-
ture. He'd passed the paperbacks on to JD and condensed the
library copies for him during sixth periods. He knew he was
one of the few kids at school who took JD's word for the
UFO sighting.

"I keep thinking about what might have happened during
the time I blacked out," JD confided. "When Stephanie was
gone. What *really* happened?"

Chic didn't say anything at first. JD's question was a dead
giveaway. He must think something *had* happened or he
wouldn't be psyched about it.

"Got any theories?" Chic asked.

"What if"—JD leaned forward, like he was getting this idea
for the first time—"what if I was taken into that UFO? You
know, and examined or injected or something? What if they
tampered with my brain? How would I ever know?"

Chic accelerated to keep the taillights of the bus in sight.
Peering through the paths made by his inefficient windshield
wipers, he hoped the snow wouldn't get any heavier before
they reached Red Butte.

"Hypnosis," Chic said, coming back to JD, who looked like
he'd been left talking to himself. "You could find out under
hypnosis, couldn't you?"

"You asked me about that before. And I thought about it.
But my chances for getting to a psychiatrist are about one in
a billion."

"Yeah, you'd have to go to Cheyenne or Denver. And
they'd charge a hundred or two before you ever got to the
couch."

Silence settled tentatively between them. The windshield
wipers continued their thumping and scraping in rhythm.
Chic was thinking. Like he'd said before, why couldn't he

hypnotize JD? He'd done it in a demonstration in health class and had put three out of five in a trance. He'd hypnotized kids at parties, just for fun. He didn't think he could hurt anyone.

"JD," Chic tried to bring it up easy.

"No, Chic, I don't think we'd better."

"See how susceptible you are? You can even read my mind!"

"Okay, so I know you've got a book on hypnotism. But you're not a doctor. Something could go wrong."

Chic detected a wavering in JD's protest. "Look! Let's do it tonight! We could pick up Stephanie. It'd be better with a third person. She can act as witness to everything and be there . . . in case."

"When we get home? You're nuts! She'll be sound asleep."

"So? We wake her up."

"Yeah, but then, where could we do it? We couldn't stay at my house. Dad would throw us out."

Chic thought a minute. He rarely took friends to his place. There were eight other kids besides him, which meant things were always a mess. Then, too, his father was either drunk or on the way most of the time.

"Let's go to the shop," Chic said finally. "The service station closed at ten. We'll just go into the back and pull down the shades." Chic had found a dozen dandy uses for the workshop where he fixed bikes and trikes and toasters and people's radios. Marvin's Garage, the establishment was called out front, but his own unobtrusive sign, chalked on a Coca-Cola blackboard, read "Chic's Cyclery." He made just enough to pay the rent and keep his car running. Some days he had grand notions about increasing his profit, then somebody would give him an old engine and he'd get hooked on rebuilding it. The bikes would sit and grow spidery until he got back to them.

"Sure," Chic went on, "let's go to the shop. It wouldn't take an hour. It's always nice and warm in there."

"What if you can't put me under?"

"What have we got to lose?"

"Okay, Wilcox, but if you mess up my subconscious . . ."

Chic went into the spasm of gleeful laughter that preceded his mad doctor routine. "Floyd Freud—heh, heh, heh!—will dissect your libido and bisect your id. He'll squeeze all the juices out of your ego, too."

"I must be crazy to do this!" JD shook his head.

Naturally, they found JD's sister in bed fast asleep when they got home, later than they expected. The school bus had slowed to a crawl the last ten miles of the storm. That gave JD time to find about seventy good reasons why they shouldn't go through with this, but Chic had vetoed all of them. "It's going to work. Just think. Relief from your anxieties. Get your head together again, old friend."

The boys pulled off their boots, then tiptoed upstairs to Stephanie's room. She definitely didn't want to be disturbed. "Shuddup," she mumbled at first, then "Go way!" with a little more force, pushing JD away. Chic started laughing. Finally, JD got her to sit up and, in whispers, told her their plan. "I'll be ri' down," she said and shoved them out the door.

JD and Chic had time to split a bottle of milk and finish a pack of soda crackers before Stephanie joined them in jeans and a sweat shirt. She was pulling a comb through her hair when she came into the kitchen. She crossed to the coat rack, lifted her parka off the hook and moved toward the back door like she'd been programmed. "Le's go," she said.

She hadn't looked at either of them. Outside she waded into the deep snow with sneakers and bare ankles without even flinching. JD poked Chic and laughed as they followed her to the car. "She's sleepwalking," he said. "I swear it! We've got her body but her brain's back on the pillow!"

The shop was just as Chic had promised. Warm. Too warm, really. Perfect for getting drowsy. The time was right, too. Middle of the night. If JD didn't resist, Chic thought, he could put him under in fifteen minutes.

Chic had JD sit in a wicker lounge chair that Tom Crawford's wife had brought in for repair and never picked up. A broad, bucketlike affair, it was the only comfortable seat in the place. Stephanie took over the high stool at the workbench, ducking to miss the overhead bulb. Chic upended a wooden crate and stationed himself directly in front of JD.

"Let me explain," Chic began, looking first at Stephanie, then at her brother. "There's no danger to you at all. You trust me, right? If you allow yourself to go into a deep sleep, you'll soon relive seeing the UFO. When we're finished, I'll simply count to three and you'll be awake."

"What if he doesn't come out of it?" Stephanie asked. Her voice was small, like the eleven-year-old she had once been, though Chic thought she looked like a woman now, sure enough.

"He'll come out of it." Chic took off his sweater and threw it over a dusty vacuum cleaner nearby. "And he'll feel good. No ill effects. I promise you that."

Chic found a chrome hub cap under the workbench and held it on his knees in front of him. "I want you to stare at this. Keep your eyes on it until you get very tired. As I talk you'll be getting very, very sleepy, and you'll soon be so drowsy you'll have to close your eyes. When you fall asleep you'll answer my questions, and afterward, on the count of three, you'll wake up.

"First, take five or six real deep breaths. Get all the old air out of your lungs."

JD did as he was told.

"Now, look right at the light reflecting off the metal. The light means sleep. Deep, wonderful, relaxing sleep. You're getting very tired now, very drowsy. You want nothing more than sleep. Deep, deep sleep. Keep your eyes on the shining reflection. When your eyes close, you'll see the light in your mind. And the reflecting light means sleep. In your subconscious, the light means sleep."

His voice droned on, repeating the same phrases. Suddenly, out of the corner of his eye, Chic caught a strange movement from Stephanie. He glanced at her just in time to see her head nod to one side, then down on her chest. Her arms had turned limp and she slumped forward on the stool. "Oh, no," he thought, "I've put Stephanie under." JD was still staring at the shiny metal, still co-operating like mad, but perfectly conscious.

Chic put down the hub cap and motioned for JD to see. "Look at that, would you?" He moved quickly over to Stephanie. He hated to interrupt the session, but she was hanging on the edge of the stool like Raggedy Ann already.

"On the count of three you'll wake up, Stephanie, and you'll feel rested and relaxed. Now I'm going to count," he said again. For some reason, dealing with her unexpected hypnosis made him nervous.

On the count of three she opened her eyes and straightened up. Chic could see by her blank expression that she hadn't the foggiest notion of what had happened. "Look, Steph," he reached for a paperback on his worktable. "I want you to turn around and read this until I get JD under. Don't stare at the hub cap and don't listen to me. You won't help us if you keep going to sleep."

"I didn't go to sleep," she was indignant. "What are you talking about?"

He swiveled her around on the stool to face the other direction. "Concentrate on that book. There's a story in there called 'The Pantomime.' You'll like it."

Chic returned to his seat on the box. "You still relaxed, JD?"

"Yeah. Let's go."

"All right, from the beginning." Chic remembered reading that anxious, nervous people made the poorest subjects. Maybe JD's present state of mind put him in that category. But Chic was surprised, after some minutes of soothing persuasion to see JD's face relax and his shoulders settle perceptibly. Seeing Stephanie go in and out of a light trance with no ill effects had made the difference, Chic decided. Now JD trusted him.

JD closed his eyes, opening them each time more slowly, with more effort, to stare at the metal. After another few minutes, his eyes failed to open and his head nodded forward.

"Now you are in a deep, deep sleep. A very relaxing sleep. You are going to go into a deeper, heavier sleep. Taking long breaths, now, you are very relaxed. You are very tired. You don't want to move. You only want to sleep."

Chic picked up JD's hand and let it fall. He turned JD's head to one side where it hung loosely over his shoulder. He was sure JD was now in a hypnotic trance. Chic looked up to see that Stephanie had turned around and was watching, wide-eyed and unbelieving. For her sake, Chic once more raised JD's hand and let it fall limply in his lap. He signaled Stephanie to stay where she was and continued in the same low, reassuring voice.

"Deep sleep . . . deeper and deeper . . . deeper and deeper sleep. Now you are going to go back, in this deep, relaxing sleep, back to that Saturday night in October, back to the night on Skull Mountain, and you will answer my questions. When I next speak to you, when I next ask you where you are, you'll be back on Skull Mountain, asleep . . . asleep with Stephanie there beside you . . . in the lean-to . . . you will answer my questions, you are back on the mountain . . . deep in sleep."

Chic changed his position, resting his arms on his knees so he was looking right in JD's face. He felt his own heart beat increase. He wished he'd had time to prepare for this. He hardly knew where to start, but his next clue came from JD himself whose face was suddenly agitated.

"No . . . I don't want to," JD said, startling Chic.

"What don't you want to do?"

"Go back on the mountain," JD answered, his voice sounding strange, unnatural.

"Yes, JD. I want you to go back to the night on Skull Mountain. You'll recall everything. Remembering it won't hurt you. Let's go back to that Saturday night—"

JD's face worked. "No! I'm afraid."

"You won't be hurt. Honest. You'll be okay. I just want you to remember everything that happened. You're there now, and Stephanie's trying to wake you up. What's she saying?"

"She's shaking me," JD said finally in a peculiar thick voice.

"Is it time to get up?" Chic asked.

"I think it's time to get up and I've overslept. The elk are starting to move."

"What's Stephanie saying?"

"She sounds scared. Real scared and she keeps saying 'Oh, God! Oh, God!' and I don't know what's wrong with her."

"Are you getting up now?"

"Yes, I'm out of the lean-to and everything's red. It's on fire!"

Suddenly JD's mouth contorted. His body jerked like he felt an actual electric shock.

"What is it?"

"I don't know. It's terrible! I'm pulling Stephanie out to see. A big . . . bright . . . like orange and red . . . a giant ball, sitting right on the power lines . . . I can't get on my boots . . ."

"What are you doing now?"

JD didn't answer. Chic repeated the question.

"I look and look. Oh, God, what is it? We're running, back to the trees. I'm trying to think what's happening. We hide and I keep pushing her off so we can run again . . ."

"Is it still there?"

JD had started to tremble. "No. Now it's moving. And we're hanging onto each other."

"Where? Where does it go?"

"It moves up. Up and then over, wobbling, closer to us, but heading for the clearing. It's so smooth. I can't believe I'm seeing it move. Now I can see the rim—around the middle. And the glow isn't like it was."

"How do you mean?"

"The lights. They're different colors now, blinking on and off and it looks like a picture of something I've seen, but it doesn't make any noise. I can't believe I'm seeing it."

"What do you think it is?"

"I think it's a UFO and I tell Stephanie and that scares her more. It's so quiet. There's no sound but humming, far away, and I think the wind's in the trees—"

"Are you still afraid?"

"Yes. But not like before. I don't think it's after us. It isn't moving now but the light's still so bright—"

"Do you stay there, hiding from it?"

"No, I think about the camera and I want to get a picture."

"Do you have the camera?"

"No, but I get up and run for it and Stephanie starts crying and holding onto my legs, but I get away and go to the lean-to. She's afraid. I feel like crying, but I have to get a picture."

"Go on—"

"I'm crouching behind the VW. The light is so bright I can see the settings, but I don't know where to set it. And I put it on infinity and close it down half way. I can't hold the camera still. I'm shaking and I think I've ruined the picture."

"Then what do you do?"

"I want to get closer. It isn't moving. It's quiet. And I start running and I'm so scared, I keep ducking down. Two more times, the UFO's in my view finder. Now I can see it better. It looks like metal, shimmering . . . but my hands are shaking so much I'm afraid to press for the picture."

At just that moment JD sat up in the chair, as if he could see something behind Chic somewhere.

"What is it? What do you see?"

"I can't go back. I'm running faster and faster and I can't stop. Stephanie's screaming and that thing, that thing is pulling me . . ."

Without warning, JD was there again. He wasn't describing what had happened. It *was* happening. He slumped down into the chair, cowering from the light, drawing himself into a ball. "No, no . . . no!" the sounds came from his throat like animal yelps. At the same time, Stephanie cried out and moved quickly to JD, but Chic grabbed her arms and held her back. "He's all right," he whispered. "You can't stop him now!" She was strong and wild-eyed, but somehow he kept her from JD.

"What is it?" Chic asked, fully as scared now as Stephanie, but unable to stop what they were doing.

JD moaned and writhed in the chair.

"What is it? Where are you?"

"Don't!" he cried, seeming not to hear Chic's voice. "Don't take me. No, no. I can't! I can't walk!" His voice, shrill and high, didn't sound like JD's at all.

"What's happening now?" Chic tried in vain to make contact with JD's subconscious. "JD! Answer me! Where are you?"

JD's face and neck were wet with perspiration. He was crying and shaking violently. Chic looked at Stephanie. He didn't know what to do.

"Count to three!" she said desperately. "Look at him, Chic. Get him out of it!"

Then JD was calling out again, in a voice laced with sheer terror. "Let me go. Get away, get away! Stephanie!" he screamed, sending shock straight up Chic's spine.

This time he couldn't keep Stephanie away. She had JD's head in her arms, holding him tight against her. "Damn it! Do something!" she yelled at Chic.

He knew he had to get hold of himself. "On the count of three," he began, forcing a steady voice, "you'll be awake. Do you hear me, JD?"

126

He was answered with a low moan.

"When I count to three you'll wake up. And you'll remember everything. One . . . you're coming back now . . . two . . . you'll be wide awake . . . three!" He clapped his hands on the third count and then repeated it. "Three!"

JD didn't move. Stephanie, kneeling beside him, gently shook his shoulder. They could see the turmoil had stopped. His face relaxed, but for the longest time he didn't open his eyes.

"You can wake up now, JD," Chic said softly. "Can you open your eyes? Can you see us?"

Slowly, as if he'd been sleeping for hours, JD opened his eyes. He straightened, rubbed his hand over his face, then looked from Stephanie to Chic. "Was I under very long?"

Stephanie turned away, looking like she might cry. Chic himself sighed with relief and took a deep breath before he answered.

"Long enough!" he said.

THIRTEEN

Stephanie hurried along the darkened street, concentrating on the whorls of snow that eddied around her feet. For a week now, since Chic had hypnotized JD, she'd been trying to get him to talk about what had happened *inside* the UFO. "I don't know," was all he'd say, or "Lay off, will you?" if she pushed too hard. Couldn't he *really* remember anything more?

They'd all agreed not to tell anyone about their experiment at Chic's place Friday night. It was too wild. Too scary. Just as Chic had said, JD *did* remember afterward, everything that happened—up to a point. That point, Stephanie realized, was where she had interfered.

Surprisingly enough, though, JD acted more like himself during the next few days than he had since Skull Mountain. His appetite seemed to return, he started teasing Stephanie again; he even got the family in hysterics one night at the dinner table, telling how Chic had shown up for gym that day in a 1920 swim suit.

And then the nightmare returned. Stephanie shuddered, remembering the chilling sounds that sent them all running to JD's room last night. He was sitting up in bed, his eyes like

glass, staring straight ahead and screaming. They'd had a terrible time waking him up. Stephanie couldn't forget how he
shook all over, how his dad held him in his arms like a little
boy. "I'm right here, JD. You're okay," he'd said, rocking him
back and forth.

By the time Stephanie arrived for work at Kay's Korners,
her face was a study in anxiety. She wondered, without really
caring, if she'd have any Christmas spirit at all this year. Even
admiring the window display she'd arranged for Kay—the
sealing wax on fancy scrolls, the candlelight flickering among
country scenes on the cards—didn't bring back the Charles
Dickensy feeling she'd had the day before when everything
seemed to be going so well.

The shop was empty when she walked in, but she could
hear Kay making noises in the back room.

"I'm here," Stephanie called, taking off her coat, glad to
have a minute to restore her public face—the one that looked
bright and cheerful whether she was or not.

Stephanie dusted off the cash register and the counters
nearby—her regular tidying up—then knelt to straighten the
Snoopy rack she'd set up the night before. Even the Christmas carols are distorted, she thought, as the music from the
public address system outside wavered and finally failed.

"God bless us, everyone!" a man blustered into the shop
behind her.

She stood quickly, turning to face him. "Oh, it's you,
Garth. Merry Christmas!"

"Where's that brother of yours?" he growled, stamping the
snow off his feet. "I've been all over looking for him!"

"Really?" Stephanie glanced at the wall clock. "He could
be on his way to work. Did you try the restaurant?"

"Just did. I probably missed him."

"Is something wrong?"

"Not yet. I wanted to talk to him about that scholarship portfolio. The other kids have theirs in. His and Chic's are the only ones left."

Mrs. Eagleton walked up the narrow aisle from the back of the shop. "Well, look who's here!"

"Hi," Garth grinned. "Figured I'd badger your help while I had a chance."

"Be my guest!" Kay winked at Stephanie. "Say, did you notice our window out front? Stephanie did that. Isn't she marvelous? I've had that merchandise in a dusty box under the cash register for a year. She found it yesterday and created that beautiful piece of nostalgia out there."

"Well, it certainly caught my eye," Garth said.

"What's all this excitement about a scholarship?" Kay asked as she pulled out a stool for Garth to sit on.

"Well . . . JD, you know, is hoping to win a National Scholastic Award. It's full tuition to any four-year college and two of our students will get it."

"Goodness, that's worth working for," Kay said. "Does he have a chance for it."

"So far. He and the Wilcox boy have been running neck to neck on grade point. Both had high scores on the ACT. But darn, he's gone to pieces over this UFO thing."

Stephanie's face became serious. "He's under an awful strain, Garth . . . Mom says he's losing weight."

"Would he come in to the counseling center and talk with me? Not that I have any magic words . . ."

"I don't know. He says it's on his mind . . . all the time," she couldn't keep her mouth from trembling.

"Oh, dear—" Kay put her arm around Stephanie, making her feel more than ever like crying.

Garth looked down, concentrating on pulling off his gloves. "At least he's getting a science paper out of it. Would you believe 'Life Possibilities on Other Planets,' Kay?"

"Now, that sounds hopeful to me!" Mrs. Eagleton said brightly, releasing Stephanie with a squeeze. "He'll be all right. You'll see!"

Stephanie wiped her eyes. She wished she could be as sure.

"Of course he will," Garth laughed. "It's the librarian he's driving crazy!" He turned abruptly to Kay. "Say, why don't I take you to dinner . . . long as I'm here."

Mrs. Eagleton made a wry face. "You might just as well! Long as you're here. Do you think you could mind the store for an hour, Stephanie?"

"Oh, sure," she forced a smile, hurrying to arrange the last of the Snoopy cards.

"Well, let me get my things, then," Kay turned and walked toward the storage room at the back, "I'll just be a minute."

Garth cleared his throat. "You going to the Christmas dance next week?" he asked, to make conversation Stephanie decided.

"I don't think so."

"The right guy hasn't asked you yet?"

"I guess."

"I can remember how much courage it took to ask a girl to a dance. Gol, I'd be sick for a week just building up to it."

Stephanie laughed.

"How's your dad? Is he feeling any better?"

"Well, off and on, you know."

"I sure hate to see him miss the winter fishing. We were going to try for the Cisco run over in Utah this year, but I guess that's out."

"He complains about it all the time, too," Stephanie said.

"He gets out his gear, looks it all over, then puts his pole and tackle box back in the shed."

Garth shook his head. "It's hard on a man who's been so active all his life."

Kay joined them, buttoning up her coat.

Garth stood. "I'll drop by to talk to your dad Sunday if I get a chance," he said.

"He'd like that."

"And tell JD," he turned back at the door, "to get to work on that portfolio if he wants to compete. I'm the guy who has to write the final recommendation—and it's gotta be honest."

Stephanie nodded soberly.

"I won't be long," Kay said, taking Stephanie's chin in her hand. "Cheer up now. Things will work out. They always do."

Then they were on their way, smiling and waving at her through the window.

Stephanie's own smile faded as she watched them walk across the street to Garth's car. At least she knew two people who were happy tonight in Red Butte. She was glad she didn't have to account for the rest.

FOURTEEN

"What are you getting Gayle for Christmas?" Sylvie asked JD as they were setting up for the Saturday night dinner hour.

JD flipped a tablecloth into place. "I haven't put my head to it."

"The jewelry salesman came in today," she smiled sweetly, sidling up to him. "Why don't you get her something *expensive*? You could buy me a trinket, too, while you're at it, for all the favors I done ya."

"He came in here?"

"No, silly! To the gift shop."

"You don't find trinkets at *that* gift shop, Sylvie."

"You know, JD, Gayle's not a cheap person. Of course I'm not either." He turned away to keep from laughing in her face.

Later, arranging the dessert cart, JD wondered what Gayle would like. The Christmas Dance next Friday would be their last time together until she got back from Arizona. He'd have to think of something fast. Last year he'd given her albums, but he hadn't gone with her very long then. Now they were practically engaged. He smiled at the prospect of Gayle wearing his ring. Then he thought of Gayle's father. He'd never stand for it. After JD's UFO encounter Mr. Evans' attitude had changed. He wasn't hostile, exactly, but he wasn't friendly, either. Suspicious, maybe. He wanted to know exactly where JD was taking Gayle and what time they'd be in. He was forever reminding Gayle to "remember she was a lady." Once he'd even asked JD if he was still getting as much mileage out of that UFO story—like it was some juvenile nonsense JD'd concocted to get attention.

But he wasn't buying the present for her father. And this Christmas he wanted more than a gift for Gayle. He wanted to say "I'll love you forever." Maybe Sylvie had a bright idea for once in her life. He'd check the gift shop when he got off work, before going to Gayle's place. The thought of finding something unique kept him going through four more hours of bus-boy service.

JD knew he'd buy the necklace as soon as he saw it. It was perfect for Gayle. The miniature turquoise squash blossom, a pendant hanging on a chain of silver beads, said exactly what he wanted it to. It was simple but beautiful. The price tag said the rest.

"Would you let me buy it in two payments?" JD asked the white-haired Mrs. Baker who ran the shop. "I could make the second one in thirty days."

"Oh, I think I might, JD," she smiled, "if it's for someone special. You're not quitting your job or leaving the country, are you?"

"No, neither. I'm stuck here."

"Then let me wrap it for you. Christmas paper?"

He nodded, pushing back the considerations that nagged for his attention somewhere around the area of his better judgment. He'd work extra hours during vacation, he told himself. He could make it up. As he left the gift shop, he spotted a $.25 lapel button that he bought for Sylvie. "Pinch me!" it screamed in hot orange letters.

With his purchases safely stashed under the front seat of the VW, JD left the Holiday Inn parking lot and headed for Gayle's house. It was a clear night. The stars were spectacular. Maybe he could talk her into going for a ride. For once he didn't feel like television in the den with Mrs. Evans popping in at ridiculous intervals to offer chips and drinks. Sometimes it was Gayle's father, retrieving a book, or other times, they'd take turns. What a bore, JD had often thought, to have to keep popping in and out like that, trying to make it look casual. "They never get to relax when I'm over," he'd said to Gayle one night. "Let's go to a movie so they can have some time off." She hadn't thought it was too funny.

Tonight, excited about the necklace and eager to see Gayle, he bounded up the stairs and attacked the doorbell with a vigor that surprised him. He hoped Gayle would answer.

"Grab your coat," he said before she could propose anything else. "We're going for a ride."

"This late? Where do you want to go?"

He stopped her questions with a kiss. "Out. Anywhere. I need to blow out the car, take her for a run. It's a beautiful night!"

"Okay," she shrugged, "I'll tell Mom."

JD found himself whistling, for the first time in ages, and the thought crossed his mind that he might just give that Christmas present to her tonight.

Once outside, Gayle chided him. "You really *are* unpredictable!" She took the hand he offered. "I was planning to make popcorn, hot, buttery popcorn, the way you like it."

"Oh, we'll stop for something later. Look at that sky, Gayle. Who could stay in on a night like this?"

"Me, for one," she shivered.

"I don't believe it. Tonight was made for lovers!"

"Oh, wow!" She made a face as he helped her into the VW.

"Besides," JD said as he swung into the driver's seat, "I need to talk to you, and I'd rather do it in private than there at the listening post."

"JD!"

"Come on, Gayle. You know how it is."

"Do you think my folks stand around to hear every word we say to each other?"

"No, you know I don't think that. But I want to be alone with you once in a while, okay? C'mon! Squeeze out a smile."

She obliged.

"I got a long dress for the Christmas dance today," she smiled again, a bonus. "It's really—"

"Sexy?"

"Are you kidding? Mother helped me pick it out. But it fits . . . *clings!* Is that better? It's red, JD, bright red velvet."

"I suppose I'll have to shine my shoes if you're going to all that trouble," he teased.

"Swell! Don't forget it."

"I'll miss you, Gayle," JD said abruptly. "Do you know we haven't been separated for almost a year—except for a few weekends?"

"I know."

"How long will you be gone?"

"Two weeks anyhow. Can you believe all that sun? Swimming every day? Shopping and lunch? I might even try to play some tennis. My cousin's promised to give a party for me, too."

"With guys?" JD felt his stomach twitch.

"Would you care?"

"You know I would."

"Then I'll say yes—with guys."

JD didn't reply to that. He knew Gayle liked to play with his feelings, but he didn't think she could get involved with someone in two weeks. She returned his jealous smirk with a bubbly laugh that made him feel better.

"You turkey!" she said, poking him.

He pushed the VW up to sixty, then sixty-five. "Listen to that engine," he cocked his head to one side, happy to be enamored of his own car.

"All I can *hear* is engine," she shouted, holding her hands over her ears. "How far do we have to go?"

"Not far." He maneuvered around a curve to the right, then accelerated into another one that bore left. "How about this? Shall we park?"

JD pulled into a view area at the top of a bluff overlooking Red Butte, ten miles away. "Remember when we found that stunned bird up here?" he asked. They had looked and looked for its nest last spring, then left it under the shelter of some sagebrush. Gayle was afraid to hold it. "It's probably diseased," she'd said, quickly hiding her hands behind her back when he'd offered.

JD pulled the car up to the railing and cut the engine. "Little bird, little bird," he said softly, reminded of the song, "in the cinnamon tree . . ."

Gayle leaned over into his arms.

"You're my little bird, aren't you?" he whispered, pulling her close. She managed a few chirps.

And then they kissed. Without any warning, the nightmare returned as soon as he closed his eyes. Like the surrender to Gayle's lips so threatened his fears that they rushed back again a hundred-strong. Instead of her face, he saw another's. Inside his own eyes burned the ones that threatened his sleep each night and seared into his consciousness a dozen times a day. He pushed her away from him, breathing hard.

"JD, what's the matter?"

"Gayle, my God, Gayle, I can't get away from it." He covered his face with his hands. "They're back. I'm kissing you, but I see *them*. Gayle, what's happening?"

"JD, you can't be talking about that UFO again!"

He shrank from her touch as she reached for him. "They're back!" he groaned.

"*Who's* back? Why do you punish yourself like this? What's the matter with you, anyway?"

"I wish I knew!" He stared at the sky, so full and bright a short while ago, and tried to pull himself back together. "Gayle, I want to tell you the rest of what happened to me on the mountain . . . when I blacked out . . . I know you hate to hear about it, I know that, but I *have* to tell you . . . ."

"Why? Why do you have to tell me? You know how I feel—"

"No, I don't think I do." He turned to face her in the darkened car. "How do you feel, Gayle? Spell it out for me."

She hesitated. "Well, I feel sorry for you, but I can't believe everything you've said happened. I just can't. I know you're honest, JD, and that's what makes it all so incredible. How can someone like you get so involved in this UFO thing?"

JD shook his head. "But it *happened* to me! I was there. I was scared out of my skull!"

"Why hasn't Stephanie gone off the deep end then? You should hear what the kids at school are saying about you, JD. They're not talking about her."

"Stephanie wasn't with me."

"What do you mean?" Gayle sounded skeptical.

"Listen," JD began gently. Inside, he was frantic trying to make her understand. "Chic hypnotized me one night a week or so ago. I went into a deep trance and I relived what happened to me during the time I thought I'd blacked out. I was taken, I was *forcibly* taken, by these . . . men? humanoids? . . . I don't know what they were, but I was lifted and dragged, screaming, into that UFO."

"Oh my God! Take me home!" She swung around in the seat.

"Gayle, listen to me!"

"No, I won't listen to these stupid stories of yours any more. Why are you doing this?"

JD leaned back against the head rest and gripped the steering wheel hard. "How can I make you believe me? I am not telling stupid stories!"

"I suppose Chic told you afterward that that's what happened to you. He'd do that, just for kicks."

"No. He didn't tell me anything. I told *him!* Ask Stephanie, she was there. Under hypnosis, I remembered it, up to where they got me inside."

Gayle looked straight ahead, not saying a word.

"Right after the camping trip," JD went on, "the night we got home, something happened over at Garth's that I didn't tell you about. I saw the inside of the UFO for just a split second. Like a picture flashed inside my head. But I knew I'd seen it before. I recognized it—instantly."

"What did it look like?" Her question was a challenge.

"I saw the room with metallic walls and ceiling, maybe aluminum. And the light in there had a bluish cast. That's all I remember. But I knew it was the interior of that thing. It wasn't something I dreamed up. Hell, Gayle, I know I was in there!"

"And these men who carried you off? Oh, JD, this is all so ridiculous. What do you think I am?" Her voice was shaking. "Do you realize how crazy this makes you sound? Do you know what one of Mom's friends said to me the other day? 'Oh, you're *that* boy's girl friend, aren't you?' It's humiliating! And it's not right! You're so caught up in this story, and now you're adding on to it. You're *drowning* in it, JD. If you could only see yourself! You've changed so much I don't even know you anymore!"

"I can't help that, Gayle. I can't live like it didn't happen. You say it embarrasses you, well, you can see what it's doing to me."

Gayle looked down at her hands, clasped together in her lap. "I'd like to go home now," she said, primly. "Would you take me home, please?"

JD turned the key in the ignition. At least he knew where Gayle stood now and where he didn't. If he wanted to keep her—and he did, how much he did!—he'd have to pretend the UFO had never existed. For her, it never had, of course.

They drove back without saying a word. Finally, entering Red Butte again, JD spoke up. "I'm sorry, Gayle," he apologized, "I'll try not to talk about it again. It's my problem, anyway."

She didn't say anything.

"Shall we stop for something to eat?" he asked. "The cafe's still open."

"Let's skip it tonight," she smiled at him, her own kind of apology. "I'm really tired."

JD couldn't tell anything from her good-night kiss. On the way home, exhausted now himself, he remembered the package under the seat. He was glad he hadn't given his present to Gayle tonight. She might have thrown it in his face.

FIFTEEN

"Why are you so quiet?" JD asked Gayle as he parked the
VW the night of the Christmas Dance.

She touched up her lipstick, the color of the new velvet
dress, in JD's car mirror. "Oh, I'm just preoccupied, that's all.
We leave so early, and I still have some packing to do."

"You seem sad," he touched her cheek.

Gayle frowned. "Well, I'm not. Let's go in."

They walked hand in hand down the long corridor and past
the cafeteria. At the door of the gym, JD leaped a foot, gripping Gayle's hand so tight she winced. The strobe light inside, flashing red and green, had attacked JD on sight.

"My God!" he thought, holding tight to Gayle in his panic.
Then his eyes adjusted to the dark and he could see the band
setting up their equipment. Quickly he checked around: the
streamers, the refreshment tables, the gold wreaths on the
wall. It was all there and he was clinging to it—the solid, familiar paraphernalia of the school dance. He started trembling, somewhere inside. He couldn't help it. He hadn't expected to see his UFO sitting smack-dab in the middle of the
gym!

By the time he'd muttered some dumb cover-up to Gayle,

she was already assessing him with a cool eye. He reddened, disgusted with himself, then hurried to help her off with her wrap.

"Your hands are like ice!" she complained.

"Sorry about that," he bent down and kissed her on the top of the head, holding her coat hard against him so she wouldn't notice the shaking.

When he came back from the coat check, JD found Gayle in earnest conversation with Garth. "Unstable," he heard her say just as he arrived. Garth looked up quickly.

"Hi there, JD! This is a pretty extravagant dance for Red Butte Consolidated, huh?" Garth put his hands in his pockets and surveyed the false ceiling sparkling above the gym floor.

"It's elegant!" Gayle agreed, completely composed.

"Say," Garth turned to JD. "What about that scholarship portfolio? Chic got his in today. You're the last one."

"I'll have time during Christmas," JD said apologetically. "I've been so darned tied up."

"Well, don't put it off," Garth warned. The music started. Couples were moving out on the floor. "Go on, let's see you dance," Garth backed away from them. "You two have a good time, you hear? I've got to police outside until everything gets underway."

JD searched Gayle's face as they began dancing, but she looked past him, without expression. He wondered what she was thinking, what she and Garth had said. "Unstable." He rolled the word over and over in his mind, stood it on end, then let it collapse into a child's heap of block letters that he couldn't read meaning into anymore. So that's what she thinks. Does she mean neurotic? He hated himself for reacting to the lights the way he had, but he couldn't help it.

Maybe he *was* losing ground, changing, like Gayle had said, so nobody knew him anymore. It wasn't hard to imagine people talking about him behind his back, clucking their tongues and shaking their heads. He knew he was living with enormous frustrations, but he hoped he wasn't getting paranoid.

If only Gayle wasn't so distant tonight, so withdrawn. He needed her sparkle, her happy laugh. Dancing, at first, they moved mechanically with the music, going through the motions of having a good time. But she was somewhere else. Where are you, Gayle? he thought. Where are you tonight, our last time together? Finally, with the mellow strains of "White Christmas," she snuggled into his neck and he felt secure again in having her in his arms. If only he could keep her there—in a slow, uncomplicated dance where everything felt good and right and natural. He didn't want the music to end.

When they stopped later for refreshments, served at tables set up under the balconies, JD again caught a signal he wasn't sure she'd meant to send.

"Do you want to leave early?" he said. "We can get a pizza . . . or talk."

Gayle helped herself to a pink frosted cake and waited for JD to ladle her a cup of hot lemonade. "No, why should I? We've never had such a fantastic school dance."

"Yeah, but you're not enjoying it. I guess you're worried about leaving me for two long weeks, huh?" His grin matched the sarcasm in his voice.

"Yes, that's it," she sarcasmed back. "I'll stop breathing if I don't see you every day."

A couple they knew moved in beside them and began to chat.

"Hi, Kim, Scotty," JD welcomed them.

"Isn't this the most?" Kim asked.

"It's gorgeous," Gayle agreed, sipping her punch.

"What's happening in the extraterrestrial world, JD?" Scott asked.

"Nothing new." JD gave Scotty a little shove into a nearby post.

"You mean you've given up on finding life out there? *You,* our Red Butte contact, our last great hope?"

JD laughed. "What's new with you, Cabbage Head?"

"Same old grind. School, basketball."

"At least JD does interesting things," Kim chided Scott. She winked as she pulled Scotty out on the floor. The combo had revived an early forties number and was amplifying it at full blast. In a minute Kim and Scotty had boogied right into the crowd.

"Want to dance?" JD put down his empty cup and swiveled a step or two toward Gayle.

"Why do you let Scott talk to you that way?" she scowled.

"What way? What'd he say?"

"That snide bit about the extraterrestrial world."

"Oh, heck, Gayle, that's just Scott."

She set down her lemonade, half-finished. "JD, let's go. If they play 'Jingle Bell Rock' one more time I'll scream!"

"What's the matter? Do you want to dance with someone else? Say so and I'll cut in—"

"No, JD. Really, let's get out of here," she pleaded. "I don't feel very well."

"Are you sick?"

"No, I'm not sick! You'd get a worried look on your face if I said I had a hangnail! I just don't feel like being here. Let's go somewhere."

"Sure," JD answered. Why not? He'd suggested it in the

first place. JD knew something had been eating at Gayle the entire week before the dance. They went along, pretending, he thought, that everything was the same as always. But it wasn't. Even so, tonight, before Gayle left with her folks for vacation, he wanted to give her the Christmas present. God, how he was going to miss her! He wondered if he'd make it through the next two weeks!

They drove around awhile, then parked in front of Gayle's. She'd turned down pizza *and* Harper's Lookout.

"My folks are in bed," she whispered, as if her dad could hear her out in the car. "Come in and I'll fix hot chocolate."

He felt in the pocket of his coat to make sure the gift box was there, then went around to open the car door for Gayle. He held her close for a minute as he helped her out, but she pulled away.

"It's cold. Let's go in," she said.

As soon as they'd laid their coats over the back of a sofa, he took her hand and put the narrow box in it. JD wasn't sure about his timing. He just knew he was excited about the silver and turquoise necklace and wanted her to see it.

"It's your Christmas present and I thought you should open it tonight . . . since you won't be here."

"Oh, JD!" her face looked funny. "Why didn't you tell me you were going to do this?"

"Christmas is for surprises, right?"

"Oh, *you!* What is it?" she led him into the kitchen where she snapped on the recessed lights.

She smiled happily, like a little girl with a birthday, he thought as she carefully took off the ribbon and the paper. But then she didn't open it. She laid it to one side.

"Go ahead," he urged.

"Then it'll all be over," she explained. "Let me enjoy the

suspense for a while, okay?" She reached in the cupboard for the chocolate mix. He shrugged.

"How could you buy me a present? Owing so much on your car?"

"I juggled the December payment. But I'll make it up. I work nearly every day during vacation."

"But won't you be in trouble at the bank?"

"Nah. It's okay. My credit's good."

A few minutes later, she was stirring the good-smelling chocolate at the stove and he was sitting at the kitchen bar watching her, enjoying the soft curves of her arm and the arch of her neck. He was glad he'd bought the necklace. Gayle was worth it. She was used to nice things and she deserved the best from him.

"JD," she interrupted his thoughts. "What made you so jumpy tonight? When we first got to the dance?"

"You don't want to hear about it, Gayle. The subject is *verboten*, remember?"

"Do you know what I think?" she slid a steaming mug across the counter for him.

"What?"

"I think you should go to Cheyenne to see a psychiatrist."

"You think I've really flipped, huh?"

"No, JD, but you will if you don't get some help."

"I've thought of it myself. Maybe it would only take once or twice. Chic told me the same thing."

"Oh, Chic! Leave him out of this. What does he know?"

"What does anybody know?" JD said under his breath. Then, sounding hopeless, "but getting to see a shrink is impossible, Gayle. Dad couldn't pay for it. Neither could I."

"Well, I suppose it was a stupid idea," Gayle looked desolate. "Have you really tried to get hold of yourself, JD? You know—just quit talking about it. Quit dwelling on it. You know you've become sort of a bore on the subject, don't you?"

JD looked at her hard. She wasn't mincing words. He poked at the marshmallow with his spoon. "Yeah, I suppose I have."

"Just tell yourself it was all a bad dream!" she suggested, her voice too bright.

"Yeah, well, it doesn't work."

A glum silence fell over them. JD wondered why he'd ever expected her to understand anything.

"JD, what you do is your own business."

He shook his head. "But what I do is *our* business, if it affects the way we are together. I know I promised not to talk about the UFO, but you brought it up."

"Well, I won't again. You can count on it." Her face had suddenly gone rigid. What was she saying?

"You don't want to have any part of my miseries," he said, his voice flat.

"No. Not now or ever."

"All right," he looked down at his cup.

"I mean," she gestured in a helpless way, "I can't see us going together any longer." She slid the unopened box over in front of him. "I think you should take this, too. I didn't buy you anything."

"Gayle!" he choked on her name.

"Please, JD, don't fight me. I can't see you anymore. I don't even want to." She stood and turned her back to him. JD struggled to control himself. He hardly knew what was going on. What was it he'd said? Why was she doing this?

"Can't we talk about it?" he finally asked, his voice sounding so weak it made him sick.

"No!" She walked out of the room and brought back his coat. "You'll have to see yourself out," she mumbled and turned her profile to him. She was like a rock. He couldn't believe it was happening. She was absolutely unfeeling.

Like someone in a daze, he put on his coat. He looked again at the Christmas present, lying forlornly on the cold counter top, then left without touching it. "Yes," he thought, "I can see myself out. I can sure do that." But the front door blurred at the end of the hallway and the door knob was harder to find than he'd supposed.

When JD got home and parked beside the darkened house, the impact of Gayle's words hit him. All the feelings, held in check by pure bewilderment, now tightened on his throat like a band. He gripped the steering wheel with both hands and gave it a yank that might have pulled it out.

"Goddamn her!" he cursed through clenched teeth, bringing his fist down hard on the dashboard. "Damn her! Damn her!" Then he put his head in his arms and sobbed.

SIXTEEN

Somehow, JD got through the holidays. It was tradition that saved him, he guessed. What else can you do, Christmas Day, when your sister still wakes you up at six o'clock to go downstairs to see the tree with her? When the smell of baking ham and hot scones fills the house to remind you of all the Christmas mornings that have gone on before?

JD was glad for the refuge. He was glad to have the sickness subside, even for one day. Although he had been preoccupied of late, he didn't fail to notice now how close their family seemed this year. His dad really liked the new reel and telescoping rod JD bought for him. Stephanie modeled the sweater he'd picked out, hugging him, spreading her appreciation all over the place. Then there was his mom's gentle reassurance that there would be happier Christmases ahead for him. Even the sun got in the act, shining like crazy that morning, making the old snow sparkle like new.

By the end of the day, however, JD could feel that he was slipping back into the same old morose pattern, and he didn't think he could stand that. He took a long walk by himself, downtown and along Center Street, past the police station and on out to the highway, then back by way of the church and the hospital which stood in disquieting proximity to one another. The brittle cold reddened his face and numbed his fingers, even inside his gloves. No one was out except the little kids trying their sleds and walkie-talkies, and Mike Butzow, looking like he was just going on duty. Naturally, JD ended up walking by Gayle's house, but he wouldn't let himself turn to look at it. He knew it was empty and would continue to be—for him. Actually, he wished he'd been scheduled to work tonight. Working, when they were busy, was the one thing that kept him from thinking about himself.

Once school had let out for Christmas vacation, JD took all the hours that Bob Gillispie would give him. Otherwise, he spent what time he had on the term paper and one of the essays for the scholarship competition. Some nights, not starting to study until ten-thirty or eleven, he found it impossible to concentrate. In the middle of writing a sentence, he'd slip back to Skull Mountain. His body would grow cold, he'd feel the strange floating sensation as he was lifted under his arms and carried away, his legs paralyzed, screaming protests that stayed in his throat and never got to be words. Then he'd force himself back to the present—clench his fists, or grind his teeth or refocus the light—whatever it took to keep his mind on the work at hand. A few minutes later, he'd see the dark figures coming at him again. He'd taken cold showers, gone jogging, even downed a few tranquillizers he bought from a kid at work.

For a while, the diversions helped. But even then, when his head mercifully gave him a rest from the UFO, Gayle appeared with her rosy cheeks and her soft hair and teasing laugh. Sometimes losing her was too much to bear. He'd gone over all the reasons he shouldn't have regrets: she was selfish —he knew it—she was vain and spoiled. But he loved her. It didn't make any sense, but he loved Gayle Evans. And like some part of his sanity, or at least his equilibrium, he feared she was lost to him forever.

It was after dark when JD got back to his own neighborhood. The wind had come up, a piercing prairie wind, that rendered his Navy pea coat about as effective as nylon net. He quickened his step. When at last he saw the lighted windows of home, he knew they were the friendliest ones in town. JD could smell the popcorn as soon as he opened the door. Stephanie was setting up the Monopoly board on the kitchen table and had apparently conned their folks into a game. They were all pulling up chairs just as he walked in.

"Count out some money for me, too, Steph," JD said, stomping his boots on the rug. Then he indulged in what he considered a justified untruth, "I feel lucky tonight."

The Saturday before school was ready to start again, JD treated himself to a day off. With all he'd spent for Christmas, he couldn't earn his car payment for this month, no matter what. Besides, he wanted to see Chic. They could shoot some pool. Just hanging around with old Wilcox would make him feel better.

Chic acted real glad to see JD, too. He even took time to show him how he'd repaired his first TV set.

"You're getting in the big money, Chic. What will you charge for this one?"

Chic made a face. "It's our own. Dad said he'd kill me if I ruined it, so, of course, I didn't."

"My friend the genius!" JD was honestly impressed. "You wanta play a game of pool? You too busy?" He looked at the staggering backlog of broken and aged clap-trap that Chic had surrounded himself with in the shop.

"No, let's go," Chic lifted his parka off a set of antlers that doubled as coat rack. "I fully subscribe to what Benjamin Franklin said," he rattled on happily. "Beware the work ethic! or, freely translated, 'A penny squandered is a penny burned!'" They left the shop laughing, JD already perking up to be with his optimistic, spontaneous goon of a friend.

They played pool that afternoon like JD couldn't remember. When they got hungry, they stopped for grilled cheese and onion sandwiches, the way only Ben Skurzynski could make them, downed a couple of root beers, then upped the stakes and started over again. They weren't good, as they'd been two years ago when they played all the time, but they had fun.

Walking home, Chic told JD they both ought to get more recreation. "Remember when we used to shoot baskets every Saturday? And when we weren't shooting baskets or pool, you were out fishing with Garth."

"Yeah, working's a real drag. I can't get out of it, though," JD kicked a rock ahead of him.

"Work and Gayle. That leaves you no time. What you need is a thirty-hour day."

"Ah, yes! Gayle!" JD hadn't thought of her all afternoon. "We broke up." JD figured Chic might as well hear it from him.

"Oh, yeah? I've heard that before."

"Well, you won't hear it again. She can't stand the sight of me. It's all over."

"What happened?"

"God, who knows? It wasn't my idea."

"You mean she just got mad?"

"Ever since October, when we saw the UFO, she's been

cooling off. I guess I'm a big humiliation to her now. I hate it, Chic. You don't know how much I miss her already."

"That's tough, JD. You've been going with her a whole year."

"Sometimes I felt like"—he wasn't sure how to say it—"we were married. You know? I mean, we were together a lot. We could almost read one another's minds. Then you start counting on each other and you think of things during the day you want to tell her . . . oh, hell! Just don't go steady, Chic! Take my word for it!"

"Yeah, I'll take your word."

Chic has the right idea, JD thought. He's so wrapped up in books and things he never thinks of girls. Or does he? JD didn't really know Chic that well anymore.

"Hey," Chic stopped and grabbed JD by the arm, "I have this terrific idea!" When Chic got a terrific idea, his whole body vibrated.

"Let's organize a UFO watch."

"You've gotta be crazy!"

"No, seriously. It'll take your mind off Gayle. We can get a couple snowmobiles and some of those giant inner tubes, build a great big old bonfire out in the boonies and have a first-class kegger."

"What's the UFO got to do with it? You think I need another UFO?"

"Don't you see? We *call* it that. Who could resist? 'Step right up, folks, and spot yourself a Flying Saucer!'" He barked it out through an imaginary megaphone.

JD couldn't believe it. Chic, hot in pursuit of the idea had already lassoed and shackled it.

"And then, with a bunch of us out there, we put our heads together and try to call one in."

"A UFO?"

"Sure."

"Wait a minute, Klutz," JD stopped and leaned against a telephone pole like he couldn't take one more step without some explanation. "How do you figure on calling one in?"

Chic poked at his head with his forefinger. "With our combined mental energy. Psychokinesis!"

"Psycho what?"

"Mind over matter! We fill the air with these pulsating electrical impulses from our brains—" he gestured out from his head with both hands, showing JD how the waves of signals would emanate into space.

"Oh, brother!" JD rolled his eyes heavenward. "I suppose I'm gonna get sucked into this."

"Of course you are! When shall we do it? When will you have a Saturday night?"

"Who knows? Look, Chic, you plan to have the whole school in on this?"

"Oh . . . a dozen or so. The *Renegade* staff, Stephanie and Carol Sue, who else?"

"It's your party."

Back on the sidewalk again, heading toward Marvin's Garage, Chic asked JD to stop by the shop a minute. "I've got an article on the Zeti Reticuli System you might want for your term paper, and I wanta show you something else."

The "something else" was what interested JD the most. Once inside, Chic pulled a map out of a drawer in the workbench. "I sent to the Geological Survey in Washington, D.C., for this."

"What is it?"

"A magnetic map of this part of Wyoming. This," Chic traced a line he'd marked in ink, "is the nearest magnetic fault line to Red Butte. And this pinpoint, almost on it, is Dougan's pasture!"

JD waited for the explanation he hoped was coming.

"You see," Chic began, "I read in this book that if you wanted to see a UFO—"

"And you want to see one!" JD interrupted, realizing for the first time how *much* Chic wanted it.

"—you should find a magnetic fault line and be there after nine o'clock at night. This guy even says choose a Wednesday or Saturday night for the greatest success."

"He sounds like a crackpot," JD said, immediately sensitive to his own ridicule.

"There's only one thing wrong with setting a date. UFO's seem to appear in waves—like an epidemic or something. And when one of these UFO flaps is on, *that's* when we should go out looking for one. But let's do it, anyway. It'll break the monotony."

"Then this *sudden* idea of yours . . ."

Chic looked sheepish. "It wasn't so sudden. I've been thinking about it for weeks." He folded the map and put it back in the drawer.

"Look, JD, you said yourself I oughta get to know Stephanie better. I can't ask her out—Mr. Ugly himself—but maybe she'd slide down the hill in my innertube," Chic said, his eyebrows jumping up and down in his forehead.

JD laughed. He didn't believe Wilcox for a minute. But he had the most inventive means of persuasion.

"Okay, ugly, you're on! Later in January, all right? I'll have to build up to it."

They locked the shop, leaving Chic's place with an early night fog moving in around them. "C'mon over for dinner," JD asked on impulse. It had been ages since Chic had eaten with them. "Stephanie's making lasagna, so there'll be plenty."

Chic grinned. "You force me into it!" he said and they started down the street toward the Anderson's.

SEVENTEEN

"Can you believe we're going to a party that starts at ten P.M.?" Stephanie asked for about the third time, wiping off her side of the windshield. She loved going tubing anytime, but late at night with all JD's friends would be more fun than ever.

"Chic doesn't do anything halfway," JD said, intent on following the cow trail that led into Dougan's pasture. "You're in the big league tonight, Steph. You and Carol Sue with a bunch of moldy old seniors."

"Well, I know why I was invited." Stephanie hinted at dark motives.

"Why?"

"Because Chic had to invite Carol Sue so her dad would let us use their place . . ."

"So?"

"So who's her best friend? One single sophomore girl at an all-night senior bust? We figured it out right away, of course —but we don't care!" She pulled on a tweedy looking stocking cap that matched her gloves.

"You know something?"

Stephanie turned to JD.

"You were the first person Chic mentioned inviting when he thought about this UFO watch."

"Oh, so I was asked because I'm your sister who also sees strange things? That's worse!"

"Sometimes, Stephanie, I worry about you."

"Yeah, well, it's mutual. Did I tell you Garth stopped me at school Friday? He said that portfolio has to be in Monday. Do you have it ready?"

"Stephanie, you're gonna make some guy a great little mother someday."

"Don't be gross. Are you finished with it?"

"No, but I will be . . . by Monday."

"Look, they've got a fire going!" Stephanie peered out through the dark. "Oh, neat!"

They pulled up behind a jeep and the Pontiac which were parked there already. Stephanie could see Chic and the others adding fuel to a barrel of fire. Once out of the car, they could hear the laughing and talking, though no one had taken to the hill yet. JD handed Stephanie the sack of wieners and buns, then hung the gallon thermos over her other arm. He got blankets out of the trunk and a box of wood and they started hiking through the deep snow of the lower pasture.

"Who comes?" Chic called as they approached the group.

"Yo!" JD hollered back.

"Stephanie!" Carol Sue ran toward them, relieving Stephanie of the thermos. "What's in this thing?"

"Hot cider. Pure hundred per cent cider. Nothing added," Stephanie said smartly. She'd always heard the seniors were big beer guzzlers. It had taken JD some time to convince her the cider wasn't merely a concession to her and Carol Sue.

"Did you find enough tubes, Chic?" JD asked, piling the wood nearby, then rubbing his hands together over the fire.

"I've got four—two regulars and two biggees. Tomlin's bringing a snowmobile later." Chic motioned up in the gully where three guys were having a snowball fight. "They've got some stuff in the jeep, they said."

A few minutes later, Chic yelled for everyone to come on over to the fire. "I want you all to know," Chic announced, "we're having EVENTS. Races and stuff. Do you want to get started? Why don't we pack the hill before everybody gets here?"

"When do the UFO's show up?" It was Elaine Caldwell, the girl on the paper staff who'd interviewed Stephanie weeks before. Laney, as JD called her, had hooked her arm in Chic's and was giving him the business.

"According to my calculations," Chic appeared to be consulting his brain, "about midnight!" Then Chic grabbed Laney with one hand and Stephanie with the other and pulled them along behind. "C'mon, Lovies, let's go get the inner tubes."

In no time at all they'd hiked up the easiest part of the gully and stood at the top of the tubing hill. It looks so neat in the moonlight, Stephanie thought, feeling like she was standing above some distant untouched moonscape. Quickly, Stephanie and Carol Sue glommed onto the giant tube, hustling to be the first in the virgin snow.

"Give us a shove, JD!" Stephanie urged from inside the tube. Then Chic and JD gave them a heave that tipped them over the crest and started them spinning and tilting wildly down the long hill. Carol Sue fell off halfway, but Stephanie clung to the tube for dear life, screaming and laughing all the way to the bottom.

"It's a blast!" she yelled back, getting dizzily to her feet. "C'mon down!"

Then everybody was on the hill, bumping and screaming and fighting to make it all the way without falling off. Stephanie had waited for Carol Sue and started back up for another trip, but JD made Carol go down with him. Then Chic got Stephanie on one of the two saucers he'd appropriated and they took off again.

It was wild and crazy. Stephanie couldn't remember when she'd had so much fun. When Fred Tomlin got there about eleven with the snowmobile, they took turns riding on the other side of the fence row, out in the field for a mile or two in the moonlight. It was eerie. The air was still and the night had a ghostly glow about it. Hanging onto Fred, feeling her stomach rise and fall with the terrain, Stephanie couldn't think of a better setting for a UFO visit. Not that she expected to see anything. It was a shared joke, the UFO watch. Even Chic would die a thousand deaths if a bright light appeared in the sky. But she couldn't help wishing, even in the face of her better judgment, that they'd see one. It had been lonely, and for JD, devastating, to be the only witnesses to a UFO landing.

When they'd first arrived, Stephanie thought some of JD's old enthusiasm was returning. Then, after a few rides down the hill and a snowball fight, he seemed to draw into himself again. Stephanie had hoped the party would be a distraction for JD, and she suspected Chic had planned it—crazy events and all—to help her brother pull himself out of the depression. Several times she'd caught JD just standing, a strange posture for him, or studying the sky with his back to the rest of them. Finally, he'd simply walked away from the tubing hill. Stephanie wasn't even sure where he'd gone.

Chic noticed, too. When Stephanie stopped to warm herself at the fire, Chic left the others and came over to where she was.

"What's with JD?" he asked.

"He's so low, Chic. I hate to see him like this." Stephanie was glad he'd asked. She actually didn't have anyone to confide in who'd understand or care as much as Chic did.

"Is it Gayle?"

"He misses her, I know."

"That pig!" he muttered.

"Do you know what she's doing?" Stephanie stamped a flat place in the snow. "She's wearing that turquoise necklace all over school. And JD still has another payment to make on it!" She closed her hands on an imaginary neck and choked the life out of it. Chic laughed and made a few appropriate gagging sounds.

Then neither of them said anything for a while. Chic added some wood to the barrel and they both stared at the flames that leaped up.

"It's the UFO, isn't it?" Chic said finally.

Stephanie nodded, not taking her eyes off the fire.

"You know," Chic began, "the night I hypnotized JD?"

She looked up at him.

"I'd have never tried that, Stephanie, if I'd known how it would turn out."

Stephanie could tell the confession was hard for Chic to make.

"He doesn't hold that against you. He told me he'd been dreaming the same things. Having it come out under hypnosis just convinced him that the dreams were true."

Chic shook his head, like he knew he had to take some of the blame. "Yeah, but I was the wise guy who did it. Chic Know-It-All Wilcox!"

"JD thought, almost from the beginning, that he was in that UFO. He says his subconscious—is that what you call it? —refuses to let him relive any more of it. I'm sure glad it won't."

"I told him he should see a shrink," Chic said. "They'd know what to do about the anxiety and all that stuff. But lately, he won't even talk about it."

"Where's JD now?" Stephanie asked.

"I don't know. He walked off in that direction." Chic shielded his eyes from the firelight, looking for JD. "I'll try to get him in a race or something. Then maybe we should roast wieners and go on home. What do you think?"

"And forget about the UFO?"

"Yeah."

"Ask JD. He worked all day. Maybe he'd just as soon."

Fred Tomlin came roaring up to the fire in the snowmobile, let off one of the guys, then started talking to Chic. In a minute he took off again.

"He's going to pick up JD," Chic explained.

Then something caught their attention. A flash of light over the hill, in the direction of the road. "What's that?" Chic asked, sounding startled. Stephanie caught her breath. Then they could see the sweep of headlights across the field as a car turned in from the main road. They looked at one another and laughed, relieved, and a little embarrassed, Stephanie thought. Who could be coming now? They weren't expecting anyone else. It was past midnight. In a few minutes, when she recognized the car, Stephanie swore under her breath and grabbed hold of Chic's sleeve.

"Is that . . ." she pointed, "who I think it is?"

"Oh, God, what's she doing here?"

They stood and watched the familiar little Fiat pull in behind the others, then saw the doors open. Two girls got out.

"Claudia's on the staff," Chic said, "but why would she be coming with Gayle?"

"I'm glad JD's not here," Stephanie whirled around to look for him again.

"Fred said he'd let him drive the cat awhile."

Everyone who had gathered to warm up stood around and watched as the two girls approached. It reminded Stephanie of a tragic scene in the Greek play they'd read at school. It was happening. It was inevitable. And no one could do anything but stand by and watch.

"Hi, you guys!" Claudia greeted them as she neared the group. "Are we too late?"

"Yeah, we're just leaving," Chic said.

Claudia gave him a dirty look. "Everybody knows Gayle," she tried again.

There was silence. Then Carol Sue, big-hearted Carol Sue, spoke up. "Yeah, hi, Gayle." It wasn't much of a welcome.

Stephanie couldn't bring herself to squeeze out anything at all. Apparently, no one else could either.

"You missed all the events," Laney moved around the fire to Claudia. "The Bar Maid's Race, the Gay Gallop, the Sinner's Slalom . . ." she named them off on her fingers.

"Oh, wow!" Claudia giggled, "we should've got here sooner!"

Gayle, acting like she'd done Claudia a big favor just to come with her, scanned the long tubing hill above them. She's looking for JD, Stephanie thought.

Then Chic surprised all of them. "Hey, Gayle, let's you and me go slidin' in one of them big inner tubes. C'mon, it won't hurt you to have a little fun!"

Stephanie thought she looked glad to be noticed, anyway. "Sure," she smiled icily.

Chic was up to something, Stephanie could see that. But when Carol Sue whispered, "What got into him?" all Stephanie did was shrug.

They'd just started the climb up the gully when JD came into view driving the snowmobile with Fred on behind. For the first time tonight, he looked like he was having fun. "Vroom . . . vroom . . ." he gunned it, making like a cycle demon, then cut the engine and sat there laughing with Fred. Stephanie ran across the snow to be the one to tell him, leaving the others by the fire.

"Hop on, Steph, I'll take you for a ride," JD said. "Don't you wish we had one of these?"

"Wait a minute," she got a firm hold on the handlebars, as if to keep him there awhile. "Claudia just came. And guess who's with her?" She didn't wait for him to guess. "Gayle!"

JD's expression hardly changed at all. "So? Gayle's here. Bully for her."

"Well," Stephanie backed off, "I thought you'd want to know."

He reached out and patted her on the head. "Thanks."

"You and Gayle seeing one another anymore?" Fred asked, sliding off from behind JD.

"Nope."

"You know who she's making out with, don't you?"

JD didn't answer.

"I heard she's hot after the new math teacher."

168

Stephanie couldn't believe it. "Mr. Parsons?" she said, laughing out loud.

"Yeah, Parsons."

"Hey, Fred, that's kinda dumb!" JD sounded disgusted.

"She eats with him in the cafeteria every chance she gets."

"Sometimes *I* eat with teachers," Stephanie said. "What does that prove?"

"Well, Chic and I saw something else, too."

JD looked strange, like the conversation was finally getting to him. "What?" he asked.

Fred stamped out fresh impressions in the snow, like he wanted to tell but didn't want to. "Oh, it wasn't anything—"

"Hey, man, come on," JD said. "You brought it up. Tell me."

Fred turned and looked behind him like Gayle might hear if he wasn't careful. "Chic and I were riding around in the Pontiac late one night and we saw her coming out of his place. Now, what would she be doing at that duplex where he lives?"

"Are you on the level?" JD's eyes narrowed. "You sure it was Gayle?"

"Dead sure. Ask Chic!"

"When was it?"

"Oh, I dunno. After Christmas. Chic said not to tell you."

"He did, huh?"

They turned to see Chic and Gayle come spinning and whirling down the hill. Gayle was screaming at the top of her lungs. They landed in a heap at the bottom and Chic helped her to her feet, telling her what fun she was having. She didn't seem to like it much.

"Come on, me hearties," Chic beckoned to the kids at the

fire, "one last challenge before the wienie roast. Gayle and I will take all comers—won't we?"

She didn't say anything, just brushed the snow off her white coat and stood there looking gorgeous in the moonlight.

"Get on, Stephanie, we're going to race them," JD said suddenly. "Can I take the snowmobile again, Tomlin?"

"Sure, sure," he waved them away. "I'll get a tube."

"We're first," JD called to Chic. Then he turned the key and revved up the engine. Stephanie wasn't sure what JD was thinking, but she climbed on, game for anything. Maybe this was his way to show Gayle he didn't care. She hoped he wasn't as mad as he looked.

"We'll wait for you at the top," JD called to Chic and Gayle as they drove up the hill and circled around into position.

"Hang on, Steph, we're going to scare the shit out of Gayle."

"JD!" Stephanie's heart started to pound.

"I'll just give her a little thrill on the way down. You know? I owe it to her." His voice was hard. "She's given me lots of thrills."

Then the four of them were at the top, lining up the tube with the front of the snowmobile, ten or so feet apart.

"Did you come out to see a UFO for yourself?" JD said to Gayle in a nasty voice.

She turned her back to him without saying a word.

"Yeah," Chic answered for her, "she's gonna lead us at the Callin' In just as soon as we eat. Aren't you, Gayle?" He took her arm, too roughly, Stephanie thought, and pulled her into the tube beside him.

The others, straggling up the gully, began to appear at the top.

"Someone shove us off!" Chic yelled as they gathered around to watch the race.

"Ready," Fred Tomlin called, raising an imaginary gun, "get set . . . go!"

Down the hill they went, nearly abreast, but with the tube soon sliding crazily ahead. Stephanie held tight to JD as he veered close to them. Then she noticed Chic had one leg over the side, slowing the tube, letting JD catch up and egging him on.

"Cheat!" she heard Gayle scream.

Stephanie ducked her head as JD plunged at the tube, turning just in time to avoid hitting it.

"JD!" she beat on his back, seeing how narrowly they'd missed a collision.

"Hang on!" JD called, this time bumping the tube to one side, causing Gayle to squeal and kick.

Then they were funneling into the bottom of the hill, still at full speed, the tube slithering from side to side in front of them.

"Watch out!" Chic yelled as Gayle was thrown off. Stephanie felt JD brake the cat and turn sharply left so he wouldn't hit her. At the same time, the snowmobile lurched forward with a will of its own and Stephanie felt the sickening crunch as Chic's body was caught under the weight of the cat. He might have screamed, too, but she heard only herself as the machine turned on its side and spun them all out of control on top of one another.

The next thing Stephanie remembered was Fred running toward them down the hill, shouting "Turn it off. Turn the key!"

She raised up, hurting all over, feeling the side of one eye swelling, but knowing somehow that she was okay. She looked for JD. Beyond them to one side, Gayle was picking herself up, muttering something Stephanie couldn't hear over the sound of the engine. Then she saw JD, his back to her, down on his knees. At least he's all right, she thought. She scooped up a handful of snow, held it against the side of her face and got to her feet, just as Fred charged past her to turn off the cat.

Then, suddenly, she realized JD was bending over Chic. And Chic wasn't moving. Before Stephanie could take a step toward them, she was surrounded.

"Are you all right?" Carol Sue reached her first. "My gosh, you scared us!"

"What was JD thinking about?" Laney asked.

"My God!" JD's voice, shaking with panic, stopped all of them. "Chic's hurt!"

There was absolute silence as everyone closed in around Chic and JD. Chic was unconscious, bleeding from his head. His parka was nearly ripped off and one leg lay out beside his body looking twisted and detached. Stephanie felt like she might throw up.

"Look what you did to him!" Gayle cried, breaking into convulsive sobs before anyone else knew what to do.

"Stephanie, apply pressure to this place on his head," Claudia had taken charge. "And somebody bring over those blankets. He's probably in shock."

"Someone has to call an ambulance," Stephanie said, remembering vividly the night they'd taken her dad to the hospital.

"You guys give me a hand—" Fred said, trying to right the snowmobile. "I'll phone for help from Dougan's. Carol Sue, come with me!" In a minute they had the cat started and were heading down the pasture road.

JD took off his coat and wrapped it around Chic. "You'd

better not," he warned Laney who looked like she might try to rearrange Chic's legs.

She pulled away on the verge of tears. "He looks so helpless. Do you think he'll be all right?"

"Oh, God, I hope so," JD's voice cracked. Stephanie thought he was going to cry as he bent over Chic's face and wiped away the blood with his bare hands.

"Come on, boy," he said softly, "I'm so sorry. Come on, Chic. Wake up. I didn't mean to hurt you. God knows I wouldn't hurt you."

Claudia was unfolding the blankets. Gently, they slid one under his back and covered him with two more.

"Get some light over here," JD called out, this time with the tears running down his cheeks. "Is there a torch or flashlight somewhere?"

The boy who had the jeep pulled it up into the pasture and parked it so the light shone across Chic's slight form. Beyond the group, the headlights cast long, sad shadows onto the tubing hill. In the gully, the fire—once intended to attract a UFO or two—died down, unattended.

Soon Stephanie could hear the wail of the ambulance in the distance, joined in minutes by the sound of the Red Butte patrol car. Mike Butzow would be coming, of course. She wondered if Chic's dad would be sober tonight or even if he'd be home. It's not fair, she thought, holding Chic's head against her knees. He's the best one of us all.

EIGHTEEN

JD woke up in a sweat. For a minute he didn't know where he was. They'd all been in the ambulance together—Chic, himself, the "men" with the burning eyes. Now he was alone, threshing out of the gauze cocoon of another nightmare. He pulled himself erect in the chair, feeling hot and aching all over, then tried to focus his eyes on something. At the end of the room he saw the circular desk isolating the nurse. He heard the rattling of a cart down the hall somewhere. So he was still in the hospital waiting room . . . and Chic was still inside someplace where they wouldn't let him go.

JD ran his hands over his hair and made an attempt to tuck in his shirt. Then he saw Chic's mother, almost hidden by the hospital philodendron next to her. She sat straight and prim, staring at the long hall leading from the waiting room.

"God," JD thought, "how long have I been asleep? I didn't even see her come in."

He stood and walked the few steps to where she sat. "Mrs. Wilcox?" he cleared his throat. "I'm sorry. I didn't know you were here. I guess I fell asleep."

"Hello, JD," she patted his hand as he sat down. "They wouldn't let me stay with him." Her mouth twisted.

"Did you see the doctor?" he asked. "Is Chic going to be okay?"

"I'm worried about his eyes. He can't see a thing. They've got his head in a big bandage now." She gripped his hand hard.

"Oh, no!" JD said. Chic blind! It couldn't happen.

"And one leg's got terrible twisted. Ripped the ligaments and everything so they're going to have to operate." She dug in her purse for a Kleenex.

JD's insides churned. He wanted to take her in his arms and rock her like a baby, she was so pitiful. Instead, he held his own arms tight across his chest, looking away while she wiped her eyes and her nose. Then he said what he knew had to come out.

"Mrs. Wilcox, it should've been me! It was my fault."

"No, no, no!" She shook her head and waved her hands in agitation. "Don't say that, JD. Chic asked first thing about you. 'Is JD okay?' he wanted to know."

"But it was stupid. What I did was so stupid!"

"The others told me how it happened. It was just kids. And sometimes kids don't have good sense. That's what I told your mother. She came over to sit with the little ones at two o'clock this morning when the hospital called and said Chic had come to."

Then they went back to their worrying, with Mrs. Wilcox staring into the hospital hallway that led to Chic's room and JD going over the accident again and again in his mind. Finally, JD stood up, shoving his hands in his pockets. "I'll ask at the desk." He had to do something. "Maybe they know more this morning."

"He's resting," the nurse answered crisply. "I believe—" she pulled at a chart on the rack—"he's scheduled for surgery on his leg tomorrow at 9:00 A.M."

"What about his eyes? Can you tell me anything?"

"No, I'm sorry. We may have a specialist in."

"When can I see him?" JD's hands gripped the edge of the desk.

"The doctor may allow visitors this afternoon. I couldn't say." She suddenly became very busy with an aide who'd just walked in, leaving JD holding onto the desk feeling foolish.

By two o'clock that afternoon JD still hadn't eaten anything. Unshaved and in the same jeans and shirt he'd worn the night before he knew he wasn't easy to look at. Mrs. Wilcox had made him have a cup of coffee with her about eleven, then she'd gone on in to be with Chic. He'd hoped she'd come back out or that Dr. Burke, in and out of Chic's room, would stop to tell him something. Chic's dad arrived about noon and he passed by JD without saying a word. When the official visiting hours finally came, JD was glad to see Stephanie and Carol Sue come into the waiting room.

"The nurse said on the phone he wouldn't be allowed visitors," Stephanie told JD in whispers, then, biting her lip, "she said he was on the critical list. Mom says you should come on home."

"Steph, I can't!"

"She says it won't help Chic if you make yourself sick."

"I've gotta stay here until we know something. God, he's my best friend and I did this to him."

Carol Sue sat down by Stephanie on the black vinyl sofa, her eyes bigger than usual. "Nobody blames you for what happened, JD. It was just a freaky thing. Even Mike Butzow said so last night, didn't he, Stephanie?"

JD went back over his own conversation with Mike after they'd raised Chic into the ambulance on the stretcher. He hadn't sounded so charitable then.

"What in the hell were you kids doin' out here at midnight, anyway?" Mike had growled.

"We were calling in UFO's," JD had said, knowing how insolent it came out.

"*UFO's?*"

"Yeah. And I got in a fit and ran down my best friend. See what you can make of that."

He'd sounded like a smart-ass all right, but he knew he'd cry otherwise.

"Get in there with him," Butzow had ordered. "We'll see the girls get home."

And then the bumpy ride out to the road and the lonely stretch to the hospital, holding Chic's limp hand in his own, wishing to God he'd never heard of an unidentified flying object.

"No, Stephanie," JD said deliberately, "tell Mom I have to stay here. I may come home tonight to sleep awhile. I want to be here tomorrow when they operate."

"Should I go home and get you a sandwich?"

"I'm not hungry."

"JD," Stephanie said suddenly, shaking his arm, "what about that scholarship stuff?"

"Oh, hell!" JD stood up and walked to the bank of windows. What a mess he'd made of everything. *Everything!* "It's not ready yet. Look," he came back and sat on the edge of the coffee table in front of Stephanie. "The papers are on my desk. Just gather it all up and give it to Garth tomorrow morning. Tell him what happened. Tell him I'm sorry."

"JD!"

"It's okay. I don't care about it. Right now I can't even *think*."

He hated to see Stephanie look so forlorn. God, she took on the troubles of the world sometimes.

"Don't worry," he added softly. "What's a scholarship? Chic may never *see* again!" His voice broke.

The girls didn't stay too long after that. JD had to admit he was as glad to see them leave as he was to see them come. After all, there wasn't anything to talk about, really.

Late Monday afternoon Chic was still sleeping off the anesthetic after the ligament surgery. Already JD, holding vigil in the hospital waiting room, felt like he'd become a full-time visitor. "I've never seen anything like it!" he overheard one nurse say to another, shaking her head to emphasize her bafflement.

JD had slept four or five hours at home, managed a shower and two meals since the accident Saturday night, and otherwise stubbornly stood by to say those first words to Chic. All day he'd hoped they'd call him down the hall. In the meantime he'd gone over and over what he'd say, wondering how he could put it all in a two-minute visit.

He glanced at the clock. Four P.M. End of visiting hours. JD felt hot tears flood his eyes. "Damn," he said under his breath, cursing the entire inhuman hospital machine. "Is Dr. Burke here?" he stalked to the desk, suddenly aggressive. "I've got to talk to him . . . or see Chic or *something!*"

"Of course." The name plate read Judy and she at least *looked* more approachable than the night nurse. "Let me see what I can find out."

A few minutes later Dr. Burke himself came into the room and shook hands with JD.

"Sorry, it's been an uphill pull with Chic," he said. "We just can't let visitors in yet. He knows you're here, if that helps. In fact, the only smile we got out of him today was when I said you'd made camp on one of our sofas."

JD grinned, feeling suddenly lighter than air.

"Actually, you could go on home," Dr. Burke pulled off his stethoscope. "Tomorrow, around two, maybe, you can see him a few minutes."

"What about his eyes, Dr. Burke?"

"We'll have a consultant here in the morning."

JD nodded. "Okay. I'll go on home then . . . if you think he'll be all right."

This time Dr. Burke smiled, his funny prune face suddenly a sunburst, and clapped his hand on JD's shoulder. "Sure. We'll take care of him. Run along now."

JD did. He ran most of the way home, his parka open and flapping against his sides. The slanted winter sun, streaking between the houses, hit his eyes like a series of semaphores. "God," he prayed earnestly, "Chic's got to see again!"

JD slowed to a walk as he neared home, trying to make out whose car it was parked in their drive behind his. Then he recognized Sylvie coming down the front walk, wearing her pink uniform under a fuzzy wrap. She stopped and waved when she saw him.

"Your mother just tried to reach you at the hospital," she said, hoisting a big purse on her shoulder.

"Why? What's up?"

"Your job's up. Up for grabs this time. Gillispie's furious because you didn't show up last night and didn't even call. He says he won't let you come back."

"Gee, nice of you to come by and break the news," he said sarcastically.

"Listen to me, JD! I've got an idea that might work if you play your cards right."

"Sylvie, honest, you're a great gal, but I could care less about Gillispie right now. I guess you know what happened to Chic—"

"Sure. Everyone's heard." She stopped talking and looked serious. "How's he doing?"

"Some better, I guess. I couldn't leave last night, that's all. I'm going back tomorrow, too. Some specialist's coming in to see about his eyes—"

"Hey, guy, look!" She tugged at the sleeve of JD's parka. "Jerry's on at five and he'll trade with you if you get over to his house before he leaves. If you show up tonight . . . and apologize . . . and make it sound like you mean it . . ." she was pleading with him.

"I can't hack it, Sylvie." He let his shoulders sag and realized he felt about a hundred years old. "Gillispie can carry on without me."

"But *I* can't," Sylvie looked miserable. "I really can't, JD. You're the best friend I have at work."

JD smiled. "Thanks for coming over. Honest."

"Here," Sylvie dug in her big bag, "take this! You'll need it." It was the bright orange lapel pin he'd given her at Christmas for a joke. "Pinch me!" it said.

"Hey, how come? What do I want with this?" He walked after her.

She flounced on ahead and got into the car. "Some day somebody will, and maybe you'll wake up. Thanks for nothin'!"

She slammed the door, then backed down the drive without giving him another glance. He'd made her plenty mad. Good old Sylvie, he thought, she's really looking out for me. But for some reason he didn't care about that either.

NINETEEN

"God, what have I done?" JD cried out to the empty house as he jammed shirts and pants and socks into the same old duffel bag he and Stephanie had camped with so few months ago. His head was like a mudpot after seeing Chic. Everything had boiled up inside until he knew he'd explode if he didn't get out of that hospital. He'd driven home like a maniac, wishing some fate would run him up a telephone pole, a fitting end for the misfit he'd become.

"Why'd they keep you away so long?" Chic had said weakly. "I begged 'em to let you come in.

"Can you see me lifting weights?" Chic managed. "The ninety-seven pound weakling?"

JD tried to laugh. "But what about your eyes?" he felt like blurting out. "Look at yourself, Chic—blind and fumbling. Because of me! I'm an ass!" he wanted to say, "a stupid, brainless, sonofabitching ass!" But he just held Chic's hand all the tighter, unable to find words for the things he'd planned to say the day before.

"We fixed ol' Gayle, didn't we?" Chic grinned.

"Yeah, we were kind of rotten, weren't we? I don't guess she'll crash any more tubing parties."

"JD, on the next *Renegade* . . . will you do my column? I don't want Tomlin to botch it fooling around."

"Sure. Don't worry about it."

"Something else. Did you get in your portfolio?" His voice is sounding tired, JD thought. "The scholarship?" Chic persisted when he didn't answer.

"Yeah, yeah, I did." Chic didn't need to know he'd missed out. Not yet.

And then, before he'd managed to get out the "I'm sorry's" that stuck in his throat, the nurse had come in and motioned for him to leave.

JD turned back at the door, frustrated with grief. "Chic," he tried again—

"I'll be okay," Chic raised his hand in an unsteady salute, "the food here's . . . terrific . . ."

JD wiped his nose on his shirt sleeve and snapped shut the duffel bag. He opened his wallet and counted thirty-four dollars. It was all he had, not enough to cover the overdue payment on his car. The yellow notice threatening repossession had come in the mail that day and now lay in a crumpled ball where he'd thrown it. Suddenly JD had no place to turn. He'd seen Dr. Burke and the man they flew in from Denver shaking their heads in the hall outside Chic's room, and he knew—he didn't have to be told by some specialist—he *knew* Chic would never see again.

Our good friend Garth, JD thought as he got into his parka and started down the stairs, where's *he* when somebody needs him so much? Or Stephanie, afraid to miss a minute of school to stand by Chic because her almighty grades might slip. Even his folks, working their lives away, too busy to care . . .

JD slammed out of the house and drove to the highway. He had no idea where he was going. He just knew he had to get out of there. Away from Red Butte, Gayle, the sight of Chic in bandages and cast . . . away from the nightly reruns of the UFO terror that were driving him nuts just as surely as the guilt he now carried for that wild, irresponsible act of violence on Chic.

"God!" he cried, letting the highway blur ahead of him, "What do I do now? What am I going to do?"

It was nearly dusk when JD pulled off the state road into the Range Study Area on Skull Mountain. He wasn't surprised to be coming back to this place. Now he wanted to drive in, all the way to the clearing, even though the road was impassable. He shivered against the knife edge of the wind as he worked open the gate and then gunned the VW into the four-foot drifts without stopping, trying to stick to the tracks made earlier by some mountain vehicle. He stalled, as he knew he would, still within sight of the main road. He couldn't go forward, he couldn't back up. He didn't even try to dig himself out.

"It's just as well," he thought, putting the bag under his arm and starting off afoot, grateful for a good pair of boots, grateful for nothing else.

"Maybe they'll be there waiting," he told himself, "they know I'm coming."

"I won't fight this time," he called aloud to the snow enshrouded mountain. "I'll go along."

His eyes watered in the wind, making rivers of frost on his cheeks.

TWENTY

LOCAL BOY STILL MISSING read a quarter-inch caption in the latest *Red Butte Times* dated June 6.

"News five months old ain't news anymore," Tom Crawford said to his wife as he left for the office that summer morning. If it hadn't been for John and Addie, and even their daughter, asking him to please run it again: "Once more," they'd say, as if the printed word kept their hopes alive from one week to the next . . .

Tom turned the key in the lock of the *Times* office and wondered what *had* happened to JD Anderson. As editor of the town weekly, he knew he'd done his best. Besides the notices every issue since JD's disappearance, there had been the pictures and a long item when Garth Magleby brought the VW back from Skull Mountain. There had been a few surprises, too, like Mrs. Eagleton paying for space to try to locate the boy and, just last week, JD's name appearing on the roster of graduates, even though he wasn't there to take the diploma.

Tom Crawford, same as other folks in Red Butte, kept in close touch with JD's family, calling often to see if they'd had so much as a word or a post card. One warm night in May, he'd walked over to the house, where Addie, her face drawn and worried, had kept his coffee cup filled until midnight. "It's been one hundred and fourteen days," she'd said. Old John himself, smoking now more than ever, coughing from one end of a conversation to the other, couldn't reconcile any of it.

"I'm making the car payments," he'd confided. "He has to come back, Tom. I can't think he'll turn up dead somewhere. But I can't understand it. Why would he do this to us? Why would he run off and not let us hear from him?"

It was Stephanie, though, who seemed to think JD's disappearance had more to do with the UFO than anyone else was willing to suggest. "I know what drove him to it," she'd offered when she brought JD's senior picture in for the *Times* to use. "If only he'd waited another day when Chic started to see again . . . but even before that, it was the UFO. It was what happened to JD on Skull Mountain . . ." she'd hesitated, frowning, then looked down at the picture she held. "Here," she shoved it across the counter to him. "I've got to get to work."

Then last night, late, Stephanie had called to ask if she and Chic Wilcox could meet him at the office first thing in the morning. "First thing" for Tom Crawford was eight o'clock, early enough to catch the June smells lifting from the grass, late enough to read the morning edition of the *Denver Post* before he left the house. He didn't expect the kids to make it until midmorning, but he was wrong. He'd hardly got into his printer's coat when he looked out through the large shop window and saw them crossing the street. Chic still limped, but he was keeping up with Stephanie, who held a paper sack in her hands like she was carrying a May basket.

"Good morning!" Tom greeted them from behind the

counter as they came in. "Just a minute here," he ransacked his desk for a pair of glasses, adjusting them on his nose as he turned around. "Never got to congratulate you on that scholarship, Chic," he reached out across the counter to take Chic's hand. "Names get all lumped together in the school awards news, but yours stood out."

"Thanks," Chic smiled.

"Yessir, local boy makes good! Okay, kids, something's afoot to get you out of bed on a summer morning like this. What have you got to tell me, Stephanie?"

"Mr. Crawford, Chic and I drove up to Skull Mountain yesterday—" her eyes were bright and she sounded out of breath, excited.

"You did, huh? Looking for clues?"

"I guess," she admitted, glancing at Chic.

"Well, did you see any sign of JD?"

Chic answered this time. "We didn't expect much, Mr. Crawford. Lenny Jones was up there in the spring where JD left the car and he didn't find anything to report. Mostly we wanted to check out that place where the UFO landed."

"The circle's still there! And almost as plain," Stephanie said.

"Well, I'll be damned!" Then Mr. Crawford gestured toward a work table farther back in his office. "C'mon around here where we can sit down. You know, by golly, I'm going to make a trip up there myself. Tell me what you saw."

"You, Chic," Stephanie suggested, "I've described it so many times."

"Well, it was just like JD said," Chic rubbed his injured knee while he talked. "Funny, though, little green shoots are coming up all over the clearing now, but there's no new growth in that spot. The ground's still depressed there. We

measured it at thirty-two feet across and took several pictures
of it. It's a true circle, all right. Something *had* to have been
there. And it must have generated tremendous heat."

"Why do you think so?"

Chic glanced first at Stephanie, then turned back to Mr.
Crawford. "Take a look at what we found," he said.

Stephanie carefully extracted something from the brown
sack, a bundle wrapped in a terry cloth towel. She opened it
with fingertips, gingerly, the way you'd handle a live grenade.

"There," she said, straightening up. "It's JD's camera that
he lost at Skull Mountain in October."

Tom Crawford stood to his feet. "Holy Mackerel!" he exclaimed, staring at Stephanie's offering like it might go off.
"That's sure enough a camera, or *was!*"

"We didn't know if we should touch it without gloves or
something," Stephanie said.

"Do you mind if *I* look at it?" Tom reached across the
table. "A man my age can afford to be reckless."

He turned it over in his hands. It was grotesque, like a sur-
realistic art object, the plastic case stretched smooth across
the back with one fold nearly hiding the range finder.

"The amazing thing is," Chic said, "the shutter still
works."

"No film could survive this. What a pity. Where'd you end
up finding it?"

"It was a couple feet inside the perimeter," Chic said.
"Buried. We uncovered it poking around with a stick."

"It was Chic's idea to search inside the landing place. He
told me all the way to the Gorge that we'd find the camera if
it was still there, but we didn't dream we'd find it where it
was. Gol, how'd it get *under* the UFO, anyway?"

Tom Crawford pulled a cigar from his pocket but didn't

bother to light it. He rolled it from one side of his mouth to another, shaking his head. "I don't know," he said. "It's a helluva mystery. I don't have any answers." Finally he set the camera back on the table. "Are you kids going to let me photograph this and run an article?"

"Oh, yes," Stephanie smiled broadly, "we hoped you would. If some way or other JD read it—" She didn't have to say more. Tom nodded.

"Could we develop my film and see if the burned ground shows up well enough to make a good print?" Chic asked. "My camera's in the car."

"Sure, you betcha," Tom rubbed his hands together, "this'll give the *Times* a regular shot in the arm, won't it? I'll have to run extra copies. Chic, you go get your camera while Stephanie and I set up for some pictures of this one. We'll get that film in the dark room right away."

Chic grabbed Stephanie's hand and squeezed it. They grinned hard at one another. "I'll be right back," he said.

"If we get a good picture of this camera, could I send a copy to Mr. Corrigan?" Stephanie asked, watching Tom Crawford as he adjusted the flood lights.

"That the man who was here talking to you kids?"

"Uh huh. He lives in Denver, I remember that . . . but how do you suppose I could find him?"

"Go through NICAP," he said, moving the lens close to the remnant of JD's camera.

"Of course! Why didn't I think of that?"

"Sure. Send a clipping, too. This's certainly evidence of *something*. We can't keep it hidden here in Red Butte."

"Then maybe," Stephanie brightened, talking more to herself than to him, "maybe if this becomes *big* news, JD will read about it somewhere."

Tom Crawford looked at Stephanie through eighty-year-old eyes, but what he saw made him feel like a kid Chic's age. She'd win out, this one. She had a lot of guts and a lot more faith than *he* did.

TWENTY-ONE

Spring that year gave way to summer with a great sigh, much as the last days of October had succumbed to the long and ravaging Wyoming winter. JD marveled at how the ruthless seasons shoved the gentler ones aside. Here, away from home, where he could no longer smell the spring coming in the succulent sage or gauge its departure by the length of the wheat, he found himself straining to read the seasons.

But tonight, JD's last on the evening shift, he was remembering clearly what a warm June night was like in Red Butte. Even the smell of exhaust and the roar of engines didn't interfere.

"Anything else, sir? Can I check your oil?" JD asked his customer.

"Nope. I'm in a hurry."

Everyone is, JD thought. Everybody in Denver's in a hurry to get some place. Then they hurry to get back again. JD slid the credit card into the machine and hustled out for the man's signature, hurrying like everyone else.

"Thank you. Come again," he called as the brown compact pulled ahead.

JD walked wearily back to the station office and zippered

out of his uniform. A glance at the clock told him the diner would be closed in an hour, although his stomach, making noises, had already reminded him.

"Eight o'clock in the morning," his boss called as JD got his billfold out of the drawer. "Don't forget."

"How could I forget?" JD said under his breath, walking up 16th Street toward the cafe where he ate at night. That was his trouble. He couldn't forget anything. He'd tried. The way Chic's mouth twisted under the bandages . . . how could you forget a thing like that? Each night, trying to put his head in order so sleep would come, he'd see them—his mom and dad, Stephanie, Chic. Gayle. He had run away and now he had to keep on running. The city was sure the right place for it. Here everyone was running. He fit in perfectly.

Sometimes, though, the shadowy figures of those he loved overtook and confronted him, brought him up short. He'd taken a walk one Saturday, trying to kill time by looking in the shop windows, when he passed some guys his age who were standing there talking and laughing. Suddenly JD caught a reflection in the glass. "Chic!" He pivoted and grabbed the kid by the arm. He pulled his hand back like he'd been burned. "Oh, I'm sorry! I thought you were someone else." He'd backed away, his face red, and hurried on down the street.

Other days it was his father who tracked him. A whiff of familiar pipe tobacco, an old sweat-stained hat that looked like the one his dad wore fishing, the sloping shoulders of a man walking ahead of him . . . It made JD sick to think his father might be tortured by the same longings he felt.

JD sighed as he stopped to wait for a red light to change. "Tomorrow and tomorrow and tomorrow," he said aloud. As always, the thinking was the hardest part. Sometimes it was just easier to talk to himself—and he'd noticed he was doing it more and more lately. Usually nothing so profound as Shakespeare. "Where's the damn toothpaste?" he might ask himself in the morning, or "Man, I'm tired!" he'd conclude at night. He couldn't worry about it. His own voice offered some distraction at least.

The only person JD talked with regularly was Mal Myers, who'd call him at the Chelsea or stop by the station when he wasn't out on a run. He liked Mal. Anyone who'd pick up a wild-eyed kid in a snowstorm, then keep track of him afterward, had to be some kind of saint.

Now, on a warm June night, it was hard to imagine he'd almost frozen to death, but JD shuddered thinking how close he'd come. He hadn't found the UFO on Skull Mountain. He hadn't even found the clearing. Later, he wondered what instincts had led him back to the state road and what kind of luck brought Mal over the mountains on a route he usually avoided.

JD remembered being slumped against the door in the hot cab of the truck. He was trying to wake up. Or come to, if he'd been unconscious. He heard the hum of the engine, then recognized red light penetrating his thin eyelids. His head began spinning and whirling through the wild patterns of fear. This time, though, they weren't carrying him along, the men with the strange eyes, they already had him—inside. He tried to cry out, but he couldn't. His whole body was screaming, but no sound came out. He begged his brain for a command . . . the eyes, the fire-eyes, burning his own . . . the men holding him down, the eyes and the fear blinding him . . . *My God, I'm going to die! I can't move!* . . . then the shiny walls bearing in . . . *Get away from me! Let me go!*

"Noooo," he moaned from deep inside himself, the sound

of his voice returning. "No!" the word erupted in a shriek of terror. His arms flailed wildly as he fought his way out of the enclosure.

"Hold on!" someone yelled. "You're okay, kid. Take it easy!" A strong arm held him back in the seat as his eyes finally focused on the lighted road ahead, then on the figure beside him.

"You all right? You awake?"

JD began to tremble. He was in a truck. It wasn't the UFO. It was the cab of a truck and the driver was holding him back against the seat. JD took a deep breath.

"Are you okay now?" the man kept saying.

JD was so weak he could scarcely nod. Then the shivering grew worse. He held his sides to stop the shaking.

"We're pulling into Cheyenne. You want off here or you wanta ride on to Denver?"

He remembered saying "Denver."

Later, Mal and another truck driver had half-carried him into a cafe, helped him into a booth, then filled him with coffee.

"I checked your billfold when we picked you up," the guy they called Mal said. "You were in a heap, you know. I could've run right over you. You going to this Hank Corrigan's? It's the only Denver address we could find on you."

Hank Corrigan. JD struggled to remember who Hank Corrigan was. Then he saw Mr. Corrigan's face and the UFO simultaneously, like a double exposure.

"No," JD blinked and tried to think what to do. "No, I'm not going to see him. Let me off . . . anywhere."

"You don't look so good. You have any people in Denver?"

"I'm looking for work," JD said, trying to concentrate. He

took a deep drink of the hot coffee. "I have money . . . for a room . . . but I need a job . . ." he stopped talking, realizing he was thinking in circles. What *was* he doing here anyway? *Why* was he going to Denver?

"I couldn't just leave him there," Mal turned aside to face the other trucker, talking as if JD weren't sitting right there in the booth with them. "The kid's not much older than my own Betty."

"Hell, I'm not gonna tell anybody," the younger guy shrugged.

"You know how it is these days," Mal went on. "A driver can lose his job for spittin' in the wind."

Afterward, back in the cab, JD found himself dozing on and off all the way into Denver. Mal had let him off at the Chelsea Hotel—a cheap place for a night or two, he'd said— and asked if he could keep in touch. JD had been there ever since.

Now, remembering that time as fresh as yesterday, JD wondered how he'd made it through all the anxiety. He'd slept around the clock at first, like he'd been drugged, waking only for a drink of water or a trip to the bathroom, then falling into bed again. With the drapes pulled, day and night were the same anyhow. When at last he began to stir, it was hunger that pulled him to his feet, ran the shower, and forced him out of his room looking for a meal.

A few days later JD found a job as kitchen help in a two-bit cafe near the Chelsea. The hand-lettered sign in the window —Help Wanted—he took for an invitation. He was sure the proprietor suspected he was on drugs—at that point his moves were purely mechanical—but he tried to be careful and clean. By the end of the month the cook had quit eyeing him and he knew the job was his forever if he wanted it. He didn't talk much. His boss liked that. He just put in his eight hours and went back to the hotel at night.

After the first week, the regular meals and the extra sleep began to work their small miracles. JD faced his day off with a feeling of expectation that surprised him. By then he desperately needed a laundromat. He also needed pencils and paper and something to read. He still hadn't told himself why he was here or what he hoped would come of it, but he missed the printed and written word. Twelve years of school habit was harder to leave behind than he'd supposed.

Back in his room with a pile of clean clothes, JD sat on his bed and began the first of many letters home. "Dear Dad," he wrote. Then he crossed that out and started again. "A letter of apology to my father." That didn't sound right either. They didn't talk that way at home. "Dearest Mom . . ."

The letter he finally wrote, that took him all afternoon, was simply addressed: Gayle. He signed it with all his love, then mailed it into a trash container on his way out of the Chelsea for dinner. He was putting Gayle away. He couldn't handle all the perversity, all the problems, at once. But dealing with them one at a time—like this—he might survive.

Not that he didn't see her everywhere he turned, even months later. Not that she wasn't still the star of his fantasies. But he knew there was nothing to build on, no point in hoping for something more than what they'd had together. It hadn't been all bad, he told himself. When you love someone, you grow a hell of a lot. You're bound to get more than you give. With this kind of reasoning—rationalizing, his psych teacher would have said—JD tried to square himself with the loss of Gayle Evans.

Squaring himself with what he'd done to Chic, however,

wasn't possible. He'd never forgive himself for that. As for the
rest . . . well, none of it was easy. Knowing he'd run out on
his family—a sick father, a sister who thought he was next to
God himself, a mother who'd cry in the night so no one
would see her grief—none of it was easy. He'd always felt con-
tempt for runaway teen-agers who split on the pretext of "getting it all together." Why can't they just work it out? he'd
wonder after watching some tear-jerker on TV. Now he
knew. Healthy people *could* work things out. Sick people
found other alternatives.

His alternative hadn't been a matter of choice. Not exactly.
He hadn't planned the running away, nor the isolation from
his family. One step at a time led him to where he was.

Now, five months later, JD thought, I'm five years older.
Half a year ago I was a kid like anybody else. A guy with all
the treats. Suddenly I'm a loner and a tag-end, grateful for a
truck driver and a librarian who talk to me.

Yes, there was also the librarian. She was Japanese and she
had lovely eyes and consistently sweet answers. He often held
his breath when she spoke because her voice was so soft. She
thought he was researching UFO's for a college paper, and JD
let her think that. Once when he'd bought lunch at the cafe
across from the library she'd had her coffee and roll at the
counter beside him; that conversation particularly he remembered.

"You are such a hard worker," she'd said in her precise way
of speaking. "You must know all about UFO's by now. You
believe in them, do you?"

"Do you?" he'd countered, never sure which foot to put
forward.

"Perhaps they do exist. But I have never seen one."

He wanted to say "*I* have." He wanted to tell this woman

with the soft eyes that he had seen one, that he'd been taken *in* one, and that he'd been in a state of hellish limbo ever since.

"Is your paper supporting?" she asked between dainty bites of sweet roll. "Or are you trying to . . . what is the word? Debunk?"

"Well," he smiled, "I'd like to say I'm objective, but that wouldn't be true. I knew someone," it seemed safer to put it that way, "who saw a UFO . . . up close . . . and it really tore him up."

"Is that so?" Her eyes searched his own. "He was sick afterward?"

"Yeah." JD felt a familiar prickling on his neck. He blushed, afraid she'd discover the truth if she didn't look away. He dipped into his bowl of soup and wished she'd stop staring at him. "Yeah, he really was sick, as you say, for a long time."

"Oh my!" She finally spoke. "That *would* make one believe."

They finished eating in silence. JD wished he could tell her what had happened to him, but he knew now that believing intellectually was not the same as believing by experience. And it was the experience itself that was messing up his life.

Back in Red Butte, JD had accepted cause and effect without question. It was clear to him that his headaches and his night terrors had resulted from whatever had happened inside the UFO. What tortured him most *since* then was the mystery surrounding the encounter, the half-veiled reality, like he was always straining at a page of print—knowing it was there, but not being able to make out the letters or the words. His logical, orderly mind—trained since childhood to accept scientific judgments and reject mystical suggestions—warred constantly with his memory, which told him without doubt that he'd been dragged into some enclosure and physically restrained. No less vivid was his memory of paralysis: imagine a brain that doesn't plug into the right circuits. Trying to reconcile these polarities within himself left JD with enormous frustrations.

In the last little while JD had tried convincing himself that he hadn't been in that much danger. He'd never know, really, but why not believe that was true? Why not believe the humanoids were just curious? Wouldn't *we* be if we landed on another planet? They *had* let him go, and they *hadn't* hurt him . . . physically. Sometimes, arguing with himself this way, JD wondered if some extraterrestrial intelligence was manipulating him, even now, easing the tensions so he wouldn't crack up. One thing he did know. His experience with the UFO was indelibly part of him, like a tattoo that can't be removed. And having admitted that fact, it somehow became less threatening.

The reading had helped, of course. At the library, where he'd taken up residence after the first few weeks, he'd found one book in particular which had begun to influence his thinking. Even finding it had been an accident. Unlikely as it sounded, the book had "jumped out" at him from the place it had been mistakenly shelved. He scoffed at the idea that he was being "directed," but the thought kept recurring.

JD read the book twice, then returned to it several more times. It was written by a young man who believed he'd been given extraordinary, even super human powers by some intelligence from outer space. His phenomenal powers of concentration had been proved before audiences and in controlled experiments. But the thing that struck JD was the fact that he didn't seem to be afraid. Though he'd had his share of ridicule, self-doubt was definitely not his hang-up. He was eager, curious, sharing his experience with anyone who would listen.

Maybe, JD concluded, he'd *made himself the victim*. He thought of a spider, rolling up in its own web, dangling dramatically from a last connecting thread. Quickly, JD brushed the image aside. Spiders weren't so stupid. Spiders wouldn't do that.

JD reached the diner that June night after work with just enough time to eat before it closed. He pushed open the door and found a seat at the counter. The waitress flipped a menu in front of him without so much as a grunt or a smile. She's no Sylvie, he told himself. JD ordered a cheeseburger, then looked around at the patrons seated at tables. Tomorrow he'd be eating earlier. The faces would all be new. The people he'd come to recognize while working the late shift would still be on their jobs. The games he'd played, speculating on how they lived, what they did to fill their days, would have to start all over again.

It was true, he admitted. He sometimes got so lonely he thought he'd die. If it was only the homesickness, he could go home. Humiliated and disgraced, he could still go home. But it was more than that. It was facing up to what he'd done, to what he'd allowed to happen. It was an encounter he couldn't avoid, but one that was still too painful to think about. Maybe he had run away looking for an earlier JD, a kid who thought the world was his lollipop. Now he knew that person didn't exist anymore. He had been exposed. Like a negative, thrust in the light. He would never be the same again.

JD finished his meal, caught an uptown bus and managed to be in bed by midnight. Setting his alarm for waking up at a new time was the most exciting thing he'd done in twenty-four hours.

"Shit!" JD said out loud as he rolled over to face the wall, "a guy could go crazy with so much stimulation."

TWENTY-TWO

The next morning, just as JD was leaving for work, the night clerk at the Chelsea motioned him over to the desk. JD frowned. He always paid for his week in advance on Mondays. *This is Sunday, isn't it?* he asked himself as he walked across the lobby.

"There's a message for you here . . . someplace," Mr. Pappas, the pock-faced clerk, searched under the counter. "I just saw it," he mumbled. Then the phone rang and JD was left waiting while Mr. Pappas answered it.

"Come on, come on," JD said under his breath, shifting his weight from one foot to another, then leaning against the desk. Who'd leave him a message, anyway? His boss? Mal Myers? Terry, who'd hired him at the cafe? The only other person who knew he stayed here was Hank Corrigan. Though they'd never managed to get together, JD had asked him for a letter of reference when he'd changed jobs. No one else knew he lived at the Chelsea.

JD was getting nervous. He'd be late to work if he missed his bus. Finally, Mr. Pappas hung up. A few seconds later, the clerk produced a note pad and tore off the top sheet.

"Here you go. The call came in last night."

"Thanks." JD took the paper but didn't read it until he was outside. It *was* from Hank Corrigan. "Call me," it said. "Important development." JD felt a lift of excitement. He wondered what Corrigan wanted. JD couldn't deny that he was eager to see him. There had been a wave of UFO sightings in the Southwest. Then, too, Hank had said on the phone months ago that he'd located Clarence and Ruth Morris and would try to get a statement from them. Maybe that was the "important development."

JD stuck the paper in his billfold and broke into a trot, running the three blocks to his bus stop. He wanted to phone Corrigan right that minute, but there wasn't time. As JD slowed to a walk, he remembered how many times he'd forced himself past that phone booth on the corner. "The Link," he called it. "Instant Cheer." The exile hearing a voice from home. But it was against the rules—his rules, anyway—to cry for help.

The longest Sunday of JD's life was just drawing to a close when he looked up to see Mal Myers pull into the station in his green Chevy.

"I hear you got a promotion," Mal called out the window, maneuvering around to the serve-yourself pump.

"Yeah," JD smiled as he walked over to the car. He always cleaned Mal's windows when he came, full service or otherwise. "Big deal, huh? Daylight hours and everything."

"I was talkin' with Joe. He says you're a dynamo. Had to put you on daytimes to keep his best customers happy."

Mal was like that, JD thought as he squeegeed the windows, always trying to make him feel good.

"Figured you'd be getting hungry about now. You wanta have dinner with me?"

"Sure," JD glanced at his watch, thinking he'd rather make the phone call he'd been waiting all day to complete. "Give me a minute to clean up first."

JD washed his hands and face, combed his hair and got back into his street clothes. He figured they'd be going somewhere for coffee and a sandwich. Sometimes Mal would pick him up for a quick beer and a pizza if he wasn't due out on a run. Either way, it wouldn't take too long, JD consoled himself.

"I don't want you to get nervous now," Mal said as JD got into his car, "but you're comin' to my house for dinner."

JD hesitated. "Well, I . . ."

"Look, our grub's better 'n that greasy spoon you eat at."

"Does your wife know I'm coming?" JD wished he could think of a way out.

"I told her and Betty I'd pick you up if I could find you. Relax, will you? We're just folks, you know?"

"Sure . . . thanks," JD smiled. Inwardly, there was no way he *could* relax. Mal himself had never questioned him. He seemed to know that JD didn't want to talk about his family or where he came from. Mostly they talked sports—Mal knew everything that was going on. Once they'd even got on the subject of UFO's, but Mal wasn't interested. *He'd* never seen one, he said, and he'd seen a powerful lot of sky.

JD wasn't worried about Mal, though. It was his wife and daughter. He knew they'd ask questions. What could he say? Should he lie, quickly make up a history to throw them off? "Where you from?" was the first thing people asked and *Wyoming* wasn't specific enough for some. "Aw, you've never been there," JD had told the kid who worked at the filling station with him. "That place is so small we count the chickens and dogs when we take census."

Much to JD's surprise, however, the Myerses didn't ask questions—not those kinds. He ended up talking about his job, the glories of living in a has-been hotel, the places he'd discovered walking around Denver. They made him the center of attention, for sure. Vivian heaped his plate twice with mashed potatoes, and Betty, who wasn't nearly as plain as her name, insisted he get the biggest piece of pie à la mode.

After dinner Mal got to talking to a neighbor who dropped by and Betty—shyly, JD thought—suggested they take a walk before it got dark. JD wondered how in the world he'd ever get away.

"You in high school?" he began, hoping she'd do most of the talking.

"I'm a junior this year. But no one ever believes me, I'm such a runt."

"Aw, you're not a runt," JD said, having mistakenly pegged her at about eighth grade.

"Sometimes I stand on my tiptoes," she giggled, stretching herself another two inches.

JD looked away. He didn't feel like playing games.

"But I can't go through life on my tiptoes . . ." she said, and it came out sounding sad. Something in her voice made JD look back at her. He noticed the set of her jaw as she studied the walk ahead of them. Then, suddenly, she smiled up at him.

"Do you remember, when you were little, how you always wanted to swing higher than anybody else?"

"Yeah." JD recalled how he and Stephanie would pump and pump trying to go over the bar.

"And how you hurried out at recess to beat everyone else to the swings?"

"That was a while ago," he said more to himself.

"I didn't tell you, because you'd think it was dumb, but I'm taking you to my favorite spot."

"You are?" JD looked around. "Where's that?"

Betty laughed. "Dear old Morton Elementary," she gestured as they reached the school playground. "I come over here a lot. It's one place, in this whole crazy neighborhood, where I can be alone."

JD found himself grinning at the girl beside him who wanted to share her schoolyard with him. "Well," he shrugged, "it's different—"

"The little kids all think you're weird, so they go somewhere else. C'mon," she headed him off toward the swings.

Funny, JD thought, how every playground *sounds* the same. The gravel crunching underfoot, the ping of a tetherball hook blowing against the pole. From somewhere behind the school came the thump, thump, thump of a basketball. JD heard it hit the rim and bounce off. He thought of Chic, practicing the reverse lay-up, too scrawny for the school team but practicing anyway. Then there came a mighty whoop as the kid behind the school made a basket. For some reason it was a beautiful and tender sound in JD's ears.

Betty offered JD the highest swing and took the one beside it for herself. He hooked his arms around the chains and gave himself a little push, leaning back, experimentally. He liked Betty, he decided. She was low key. A nice change. But what she came out with next caught him completely off guard.

"I ran away from home myself last year. I know what it's like."

Slowly, JD stopped his swing. He felt his face getting hot. *Don't panic! She's telling you, she isn't asking you.*

The silence stiffened between them.

"What made you come back?" JD gave her a straight look this time.

"The cops."

He didn't say anything.

"I'm glad they did . . . now," she went on. "My mother was a wreck and Dad had lost his job, looking for me. He'd leave the freeway, you know, and drive through towns. He'd come in late on every run. They fired him."

"You okay now?" JD ventured. He didn't plan to talk about himself.

"Sometimes it's hard," she twisted her swing sideways away from him, looking across the playground somewhere, "but I'm in a new school. I have new friends."

"I should think you'd have a lot of friends," JD said, admiring her openness and the easy way she talked.

"Thanks." She pushed off, looking happy again, letting her hair fly back like a little girl's. "I'll make it!"

In a minute JD had caught up with her, glad to be free of the conversation. "Shall we top over?" he challenged her, pulling at the chains to pump higher and higher. They both started to laugh. Finally, squealing, Betty was forced to give up. JD leaned back and let the sky rock crazily overhead. He hadn't felt so good in a long time.

Afterward, having worked over the jungle gym and the chinning bars, JD and Betty stretched out on a teeter-totter apiece—their feet against the hand grips—staring at a washed-out sunset.

"I don't know why you split in the first place," JD spoke finally "and it's none of my business, but I want to tell you something. What happened to me back home, last fall, was so crazy I can't talk about it. You understand?"

"I think so." She turned to look at him.

"I—" JD was picking his words with care, "*had* to leave. To figure things out, I guess."

"But you're all right now, aren't you?"

"In the words of Betty Myers," JD said wryly, "I'll make it." He was trying on that idea for the first time. He liked the feel of it. "Yeah, I think I'll make it," he repeated.

JD sat up. "You know? I probably could tell *you*. You're the kind of girl who'd listen . . ." He felt himself wanting to, wanting suddenly to share all his misery: the nights of terror, the loneliness, the dreary sweeping up of the pieces, one at a time—discarding what didn't fit and clinging to what did—trying to explain an inexplicable truth so he could accept it himself . . .

Then Betty reached over and touched his arm. "If you ever want to tell me, I'll listen. I promise."

JD didn't tell her anything, but he believed her. It was enough for now. He stood, waited for her, then walked back across the playground, his hands thrust deep in his pockets.

A little later, back at the house, Mal offered to drive JD home whenever he was ready. "But only when you can't stay any longer," he insisted.

"I guess I should go. I've got a lot of things to do tonight." He looked apologetically at Betty, not sure if she believed him.

"I have a biology report to work on myself," she said, as if to let him off the hook. "Come home with Dad again," Betty smiled at the door a few minutes later.

"Hey, I'll do it," JD promised. Then turning to Vivian, "You sure make good fried chicken, as good as my mom's—"

It was out of his mouth before he knew it. His ears heard the words before his mind had given approval to say them.

Quickly, he hurried out to the car with Mal, an oversized lump filling his throat.

"Why don't you let me out here?" JD said, half a mile from his hotel. "I need to jog a little."

"You sure?"

"Yeah, man, I gained three pounds tonight at your house."

"I believe it!" Mal laughed as he pulled to the curb. "Well, see you next time . . . I take a rig into Des Moines tomorrow."

"Thanks a lot, Mal," JD said as he closed the car door behind him. "Take care."

JD stood and waved, waiting for Mal's Chevy to disappear in the traffic. He checked his pocketful of coins, then moved on up the street toward the phone booth. On the way JD retrieved the folded paper from his billfold. He tried to read the phone number, but it was too dark outside now to see it. He walked faster, hoping he hadn't delayed too long. If Hank had wanted to see him that day, he was out of luck already.

JD was relieved to see the phone booth ahead of him was empty. At least he wouldn't have to stand around and wait. He closed the door, blinking against the sudden light. He smoothed the paper out on the little shelf, inserted the coin and dialed the number. The phone rang and rang. "No one's home. I'm too late," he said. Then he tried again, checking the numbers as he dialed. His hopes faded with each successive ring. It was clear no one was going to answer.

JD slid the door open until the light went off; he stood there in the dark. The booth became a decompression chamber, his expectations seeping away, leaving a great emptiness inside. Now, even the car lights that caught on the booth de-

pressed him. People, together, going places. Like Mal
. . . Betty . . . people going home to be with one another.
In all the world, he alone was *alone*.

He couldn't remember, later, actually making a decision.
But he must have. Suddenly he was holding the phone again,
feeding in the coins as the operator asked for them, a dollar
fifty-five in all, for a long distance call to Red Butte, Wyoming. And, suddenly, JD was smiling all over his face. The
phone was ringing—in his own house—and he could hear it
just as plain as if he were there in the living room. He held
his breath.

"Hello." It was Stephanie. He knew it would be Stephanie!
"Hello," she repeated, louder. "Who is it, please?" He bit his
lower lip. Then she turned to someone else. "No one answers," he heard her say. Then there was laughing and
muffled sound in the background. Finally another voice was
on the line. "Hello-hello-hello-hello!" it came, rapid-fire. It
was Chic! Good old Chic! "Now speak up, you hear? We is
waitin' on you . . . are you shy?" Chic teased. "You're a shy
person, aren't you? Too bashful to say a word. Tsk, tsk!"
JD's grin filled in the pause. Then, losing patience, Chic
began tapping on the phone, whistling. JD could hear
Stephanie urging him to hang up.

"It is now three minutes, sir," the operator broke in,
startling JD. He hadn't expected this to happen. "Please notify when you are through."

"Hey, is this long distance?" he heard Chic ask.

"Would you please notify when through?" the methodical
voice repeated.

"Stephanie, it's a long distance call. Maybe it's—"

"Are you there, sir? Do you wish to complete your call?"

JD's heart pounded. He couldn't keep on with the masquerade.

"JD, come home!" came a frantic cry from his sister. "Please come home!"

Chills raced down his arms. Quickly, JD set the phone back on the hook. He leaned against the side of the booth and closed his eyes, giving in to an all-encompassing sob. For that little while he'd been back in Red Butte, in his own home. For three minutes they'd all been there together, and in spite of himself, he'd given them a message. They knew! He'd heard Stephanie cry for him to come home! And he'd heard Chic laugh. He'd sounded terrific, like the old Chic!

Suddenly JD wanted to call them all—his mom and dad, Garth, Sylvie. He wanted to talk to everybody in Red Butte. What would old Butzow do if JD got him on the phone? Or Tom Crawford? "Listen, close, Mr. Editor—"

JD yanked open the door of the phone booth and ran down the street. He could see his dad's face. He could feel his mother's arms around his neck as she welcomed him back. He'd find himself a job. Maybe he could still apply at the University.

So what if they called him a deserter? He knew what had happened to him, even if he didn't know why. And if he had to say "to hell with how it seemed to anyone else," well, he'd just have to say it. He was going home to Red Butte and nothing else mattered!

JD stopped at the steps of the Chelsea and leaned against the railing, gasping for breath. He wiped his wet face with his hands, not caring if anyone saw. Allowing himself one great sigh that emptied his fears into the night air like ghosts, JD looked up at the sky. Once again, he found himself straining to see the stars from downtown Denver. As usual, they were obliterated. Any passing UFO's or similarly compelling displays in the universe were likewise upstaged by the Denver glitter. The heavens from where he stood were all one monotonous reflection.

JD threw back his head and laughed. Tonight he didn't care. He was going home! In Red Butte, he could see the sky again at least.

Raised as the youngest of a large family in rural Nebraska, IVY RUCKMAN graduated from Hastings College, did post-graduate work at the University of Utah, and has taught English and creative writing to young people.

Ms. Ruckman remembers her childhood during the Depression years as a time when material wealth was scarce, but anything was possible through imagination. She and her older brother created a vivid world of make-believe, and today she feels that this childhood experience with fantasy forms a kind of "reservoir" on which she draws as a writer.

Today she devotes herself full time to writing fiction and lives in Salt Lake City, Utah, with her husband and three children, all enthusiasts of outdoor sports including swimming, skiing, camping and mountain climbing.